the crooked
heart *of* mercy

the crooked heart *of* mercy

BILLIE LIVINGSTON

wm

WILLIAM MORROW
An Imprint of HarperCollins*Publishers*

FIRST EDITION

Designed by Diahann Sturge

Published simultaneously in Canada by Random House Canada, a division of Penguin Random House Group, Ltd.

Library of Congress Cataloging-in-Publication Data has been applied for.

ISBN 978-0-06-241377-2

16 17 18 19 20 OV/RRD 10 9 8 7 6 5 4 3 2 1

For Sweet Timothy
Always, you help me to believe

'O look, look in the mirror,
O look in your distress:
Life remains a blessing
Although you cannot bless.

'O stand, stand at the window
As the tears scald and start;
You shall love your crooked neighbour
With your crooked heart.'

—W. H. Auden, "As I Walked Out One Evening"

the crooked heart of mercy

ONE

Ben

"D o you know what day it is today?"

The man just got here and he wants to know what day it is. A day late and a dollar short? A cold day in hell? It is a timeless question—it suits the room. A white, white room. White as a scream, floor to ceiling, bed to nightstand. Maybe it's supposed to feel clean. It feels more like we're locked in an instant that never ends.

"Can you tell me your name?"

When you say *you*, do you mean *you*? Or him? Do you mean Ben? Benjamin?

"Which do you prefer? Can I call you Ben? Do you know how you ended up with those bandages on your head, Ben?"

Dr. Lambert wants to know about the hole. Ben's black hole. If he stuck his finger in, surely Lambert could find the answer in there. How did the hole come to be? That's the question. They shot him. Boy, they did. The boy did. Meant it too. Muzzle to the head. And then he was dead. Bullet in.

Bullet out—now that was cheating. He shouldn't be above-ground. It's not a trampoline down there. It's hell. You get what you deserve. Don'tcha think, Doctor?

"Is that what you think?"

Lambert is not the kind of doctor who puts Humpty back together. He's the kind who roots around in your brains until they dribble out your mouth, the kind who sidles up with phony, fool-blue eyes, and then tries to muscle into the black hole. Go ahead, buddy. Nothing but tar in there.

"Not many survive a gunshot to the head," Lambert says. "What do you make of that?"

Survive? Who survived? Just because you save the body doesn't mean you save the man. Shell's empty. The chicken's gone.

"Hm," Lambert says. "So I'm talking to a shell. Where is Ben?"

Wandering in the desert.

"So who am I talking to?"

That Lambert, he's a crafty sonuvabitch. Give him that.

The doctor shifts in his chair, like we're about to go for a long drive. "Why don't you tell me how your body got here, and we'll get to your self later."

Self. Is that like a soul?

Joke's on him. How does anyone get here? Let the black hole speak:

Ben should be with his wife and kid. That's where he should be now. But he killed them and they killed him right back. First off: He should have manned up and gone to work on his birthday.

Lambert's got a face like a graveyard when he says, "Why

don't we talk about that. You're employed as a chauffeur, is that correct?"

Correct.

Ben was driver to the stars and the wish-they-were-stars. Made an extra buck where he could. Maggie cleaned apartments. Fifteen bucks an hour. Oldsters mostly. The old ladies loved Maggie. They wanted to give her the world, but all they had was Medicare. So they tipped with pills instead. Old vials of Percocet, Xanax . . . Ben would sell them to the hungry selves in the backseats. Few bucks here and there. Enough to keep the lights on.

Then Ben's thirty-fifth rolled around. The limo service wouldn't give him the night off so he called in sick.

Ben and Maggie had a little birthday party in the living room. After the baby went to sleep. It's hard to get a two-year-old to bed.

They did it though, got him settled and closed the door. Put on a little music. Happy birthday! Let's get high! Couldn't afford weed, so they popped some old lady's Xanax. Poured a bit of wine. A perfect night, the way the breeze blew the curtains, the moon shone through the window. Ben and Maggie dancing. Just the two of them floating in the kitchen. Dancing, dancing. Hands against the moon.

"Dancing in the moonlight," Lambert says. "It sounds like—"

What? No. Not out loud. That wasn't supposed to be for you. That was not a story for the white, white room. That's Ben's story, Ben's fuckup. Ruination. Ben is banished. And everyone's better off for it.

Maggie

How do you fill a hole? If you take from the whole to fill a hole, is anything made whole? Ben said that. It made the kind of sense that convinced me to leave him. Ben had an interesting mind. Before he lost it.

Across the street, enormous claw-fisted diggers are excavating, wrenching up earth and stone, shoveling pits and building mountains. It's not quite 10 A.M. and here I sit in a bus shelter, killing time until it *is* quite 10 A.M. You would think that I'd have learned to fill each moment so that I am never left to dig around in my own dirt like this. Every pause in the day is another chance to stare into the cavern.

My gaze settles on the arm of a big yellow digger. Like some prehistoric beast, the machine roars and stutters over the hole as though it knows that one false move could send it tumbling down into the void it created.

According to my watch, the time is now ten o'clock on the

nose. I step out of the bus shelter, look at the relentless blue sky for a moment, and then head up the walkway toward the high-rise that has been looming behind me.

I buzz 1414. A few moments later, music cuts through the crackling intercom and a woman's voice shouts, "Yes? Sorry, what?"

"Lucinda? This is Maggie, I'm here for—" A high-pitched squeal cuts through the speaker and the front door unlocks.

Inside, gold-specked cream linoleum lines the floor. Taking up most of the tiny lobby is a cast stone fountain the size of a Volkswagen Bug, its grinning cherub dancing with an openmouthed fish under one arm. Water must have animated the thing at one time, spouted from that fish's lips, but now it lies parched in that stone toddler's arms, over a dry basin.

The lobby walls are papered with gold and blue textured paisley. Straight ahead sits an elevator.

Pressing the call button, I stare back at the big dry fountain and can't help but think of a run-down Vegas casino. Perhaps, back before I was born, this building was home to many a swinging singles pad.

The elevator arrives and the doors roll open.

A flock of black birds erupt in my belly as I move up the shaft. Planting my feet I exhale slowly and concentrate on the numbers overhead. It's still hard to ride in an elevator. Rising and falling feel too much alike.

The elevator shudders to a rest and the car opens on the fourteenth floor to the same gold and blue paisley wallpaper that lined the lobby.

I step out and listen to the compartments of life around me.

From under a door on my right, canned laughter scratches its way out. To my left, the distant tinny wail of the music I heard on the intercom. My heels sink in the soft floor and I look down to see more decor from another era: shag carpet, charcoal with ribbons of royal blue.

Turning back to the mirrored elevator doors, I check my reflection, fill my lungs, and try to find the muscles in my face that will give me the bright buoyant look I'll need if I'm going to get this job. Nobody wants to hire misery, least of all old people. I rehearse the words from my online advertisement: *My name is Maggie. I have two years' experience cheerfully cleaning homes* . . . I pat my shirt collar flat and head left down the hall.

Scanning the door numbers, I come closer to the sound of harmonicas and guitars until I am face-to-face with 1414, listening to Willie Nelson sing "All of Me."

I knock and wait. Ben's father liked to listen to country music. I push that prejudice aside and give the door another hard rap.

From inside: "Just a second!" followed by the clearing of a throat. And then a hack and a louder, more insistent throatclearing.

Staring down at the shag pile, the way fibers nose the toes of my shoes, I work at my facial expression again. I recently heard someone on afternoon television claim that smiling elevates the mood and reduces stress, gets neurons firing in the brain. They said that even the neurons in an observer's brain would light up as if he were smiling himself. Faking it works just as well.

The rent on my dingy little apartment is due. I am willing to fake it.

The door opens and Willie's nasal warbling floods over me: *Your goodbyes left me with eyes that cry and I know that I'm no good without you.*

Standing just inside, a small, creased woman keeps one hand on the doorknob, the other on her walker. Her hair is short and choppy as though she cut it herself. The scent of White Shoulders drifts. Hunched forward slightly, she opens the door wider. "Are you Maggie?"

I extend my hand. "Yes. Hello." I raise my voice over the music. "Are you Lucinda?"

"I go by Lucy. Come in." She jerks her head over her shoulder, turns her walker around, and heads toward a small dining area near the kitchen. I close the door and follow.

She shoves her walker off to the side and plants herself in one of the blue vinyl and chrome dining chairs. She picks up a remote control—"I like having my music on. It's better than listening to that racket outside"—points it at the television, and lowers the volume about ten points just as a new song begins. There is nothing on the screen but the name of the song and artist: "It's Only a Paper Moon," Jim Reeves.

"Did I say 'Lucinda' when I called?" she asks. "I guess I do that sometimes. Sounds more proper, but I don't really like it. I always know it's someone I don't want to talk to when they call me Lucinda. Government people."

I fold myself into the chair, kitty-corner to her. The apartment rug is beige and tan, a little beat-up, with crumbs and bits of paper here and there. The walls look as though they haven't been painted in a good fifteen, twenty years. Lucy adjusts her glasses and looks down at a printout of my online housekeeping ad, the top sheet of a slim stack sitting in front of her. Picking up a palm-size magnifying glass, she studies my photo, comparing it to the face now in front of her. Eventually, she begins to reread the text under the picture.

I watch her lips move for a couple of moments and then I look down at the small table's Formica. "I like this dinette set. It's kind of cool," I offer.

One of my old ladies on the west side used to love to hear that she was cool. She'd want an assessment each time I picked her up for a doctor's appointment. "Do you think I look with-it in this outfit?" she would say. She loved little kids, so sometimes I'd bring Frankie with me and she'd hold up two blouses and ask him, "Which one is the coolest, Mr. Man?" Frankie would giggle and cover his mouth with both hands. Just about everything made that kid laugh.

"The young ones love this table," Lucy tells me and taps a thick fingernail on the surface.

Her voice pulls me back into the room. *Focus. You are going to get this job.* God knows I need it. I need the money, but I also need the push and shove of work in my life. Can't depend on Ben. He can't help himself now, never mind me.

"I've had the damn thing forty years. Pretty good shape except for that little burn mark. Lloyd used to smoke. But I don't have to put up with that anymore." She winks at me as though it's an inside joke. "We're separated. How about you, you got a husband?"

"Yes. I mean, yes, we're separated too." The words clunk off my teeth. I wonder if I look as phony as I feel.

"He's not dead, is he?"

My gut seizes. No, Ben is not dead. He wants to be, but for now he is not.

"Mine is. Two years now. But I don't believe in 'dead.' I believe in till-we-meet-again. How many people do you work for?"

"Ah, I have—I used to have about six households, ah, clients, and then there was—I had some—" I had this rehearsed but now the euphemisms are all gone. "We had a family emerg—" That's not the word. "A family tragedy. I couldn't take care of work and—and the family—my husband. He and I have since separated and I've decided that it's time I got back into the workforce. I can give you several references." I open my purse and take out a list of names, set it down in front of her. "These are all people I worked for. They had to replace me. I mean, they couldn't do without, ah, although, one of them, Mary, might—" Oh Christ, shut up. Nobody wants to hear what happened. Nobody knows what the hell to do with it.

Lucy moves her magnifying glass over the list of references and then goes back to my advertisement and reads aloud: *"I have two years' experience cheerfully cleaning homes for an array of clients. I am happy to take care of your errands or take you to appointments. I'm a reliable person, and I particularly enjoy taking care of the needs of seniors. . . ."* She looks up. "You *enjoy* taking care of seniors?"

"Yes. I like feeling helpful. Useful. I like to hear about people's pasts."

She snorts. "Do you have kids?"

Before I can retrieve the correct response, she shoves her little stack of papers to the side and reveals a children's picture book. Turning it around, she slides it over. "I thought if you had kids, I was going to show you my book. *Pennywhistle Pig*."

In front of me now is a bright pink pig dancing on the large glossy hardcover. Standing on his hind legs, he grins and plays a pennywhistle to a family of skunks.

"It won a silver medal in the Strawberry Shortcake Awards! See, here's my author photo." Lucy takes the book out of my hands and opens to the back flap. "That's the guy who did the illustrations." She pokes at the picture below and then flips back to page one. "Came out about ten years ago. Still sells though. Want to read a little?"

She sets the book back in front of me, open to that rosy pig sitting on his veranda, drinking a glass of orange juice. *Pennywhistle, Pennywhistle, Pennywhistle Pig,* I read, and then I feel a soft hint of breath in my ear. Milky, warm breath. The sense of it sends a shudder down my back. Oh Jesus. Not now.

The text blurs. I keep my face pointed at the page.

"Out loud!" Lucy insists.

Focused on that grinning pig, I try again. *"Pennywhistle, Pennywhistle, Pennywhistle Pig."* And then stop. The weight of him, the feel of his movement. Jesus Christ, it's happening. I can feel his little bum in my lap, his warm back against my chest. Ghostly and real at once, the way I feel him in the twilight between sleep and waking, the whole of me curved around my Frankie before I open my eyes and find the truth of my life. Christ, make this go away. My lap is empty, and yet he is here, the sway of him. A part of me believes if I move quickly enough, I'll catch my child waiting on the other side of some invisible membrane.

Breathe. Cheerful. Smile, smiling . . . elevates mood . . . neurons firing.

I will my cheeks up, push them right to the eyes, my mouth spread in some ghastly imitation of cheer, of someone you'd want to have around.

I start again:

"Pennywhistle, Pennywhistle, Pennywhistle Pig,
saw the folks across the road begin to dance a jig."

"See it's all in rhyme," Lucy says. "Hardly anyone has the rhythm it takes to write in rhyme, but I've got it. The publisher said I'm the best they ever saw. Carry on."

The shudder has moved into my limbs. The page shakes as it turns. *"Pennywhistle whispered—"* My throat closes and I pause as I feel the fat, rolling tear slip off my jaw and land in a splat.

Lucy recoils. She bends forward, dabs a finger on the page. "What's that?" She takes the book from my hands and peers up at the ceiling.

My head stays down. Frozen. "I'm sorry," I whisper. "I'm so sorry."

Lucy looks from her book to my face. "You're crying? Oh, for God's sake." She sounds agitated, reaches down into the basket at her walker's base. Snatching a handful of tissues, she pushes one into my hand and wipes the page of the book with another.

I wipe my eyes and nose. "I'm sorry. I'll pay for it." I unzip my purse. "I'll just pay for this and then I'll go."

"No, no. It's fine. Don't be silly. I guess you've got—you must be going through a hard time. Your husband's dead, but that's not the end. The way I—"

"He's not dead. He's here. He's—" It's all tumbling out of my mouth and it's got to stop.

I get up from the table. "I'm sorry. I have to go. I'm sorry."

Seconds later I am rushing down the hall, tears streaming. I'm sorry I'm sorry I'm sorry.

Ben

D r. Lambert is back again. "I had hoped to see you in
the common room today," he says. "It was a good group
session."

He leans forward a little. Here it comes; he is about to say
something *meaningful*.

"The dark place a person finds himself," he says, "that sadness can be tremendous, but there were people in that room
today who were also in a lot of pain. I know that you might
not feel like being around others at this point, but participa-
tion in a group can provide a kind of permission to express
your sadness and work through it—which not only helps you,
it helps others."

Heaven help the others. God help us. The Lord helps
them that help themselves. Some men are beyond help. I got
a brother-in-law in the God business . . . riding both sides of
the fence. Where does that leave us? Where does that leave
you, Doctor?

Lambert sits back in his chair. He waits. Lambert and the white room breathe in sync. Finally he says, "It sounds as though you and your wife separated shortly after your birthday."

That's right. She'd rather be with no man, than a man like Ben.

"Why don't we try and talk about that night. Dancing in moonlight . . . your description yesterday, it sounded as though you were very much in love with Maggie."

Ben and Maggie in love. Very much in love.

Ben and Maggie, Maggie and Ben, dancing away, their last night as a couple: just the two of them floating in the kitchen. Maggie had been working her ass off all day, hauling old ladies to geriatric clinics and denturists, making their beds, vacuuming their floors, filling their goddamn hummingbird feeders . . . one long day of gimme-gimme-gimme. Ben had been home with Frankie and he spent most of it pulling him off the ceiling. Two-year-olds: That's just how it is sometimes.

Tucking that kid into bed and then slipping into that soothing quiet together was such a sweet relief.

"Soothing quiet." Lambert looks down at his notes. "Was it common for the two of you to use sedatives as a recreational drug?"

Common for *what*? One of the old ladies gave the pills to Maggie as a tip. Mrs. Riley. She used to complain that her doctor didn't listen, he prescribed: sleeping pills, anti-anxiety meds, painkillers. That's what they do with old people: pill them up to shut them up. Mrs. Riley had the prescriptions filled, but she never took the pills—maybe a Percocet now and then, for her back. Her medicine cabinet was crammed with bottles, going back ten years. She didn't have much money, so once a month or so, she'd give Maggie something as an extra thank-you. Maggie gave them to Ben and Ben sold them to limo clients. The night before his birthday he unloaded most of the Xanax on some tweaked-out stockbroker. A hundred bucks for the pills and a hundred in tips. Ben stopped at the twenty-four-hour supermarket on the way home and bought groceries and a cheap bottle of wine for his birthday. He paid the electric and phone bills in the morning. That's the kind of *recreation* they usually got from Xanax.

That day was a real ballbuster for both of them. By dinnertime they were both fed-up and bitched out. The Xanax was Ben's idea. It was his birthday. He had two left in the bottle and he wanted to chill with his wife. So that's what they did. They had a glass of wine and slipped into that heart-shaped bubble and danced. They stared into one another's eyes for the first time in weeks.

Everything was going to be okay. They were going to make out just fine. As soon as that thought entered his mind, Ben should have bolted the doors and barred the windows.

Maggie and Ben, just the two of them floating in the kitchen.

And then suddenly the baby: Little Frankie climbing up the couch.

Standing on the windowsill, hands against the moon. As if he would be taken up. It was a vision. Small hands on the window, pushing until it opened into the night, into the universe. Ashes ashes, we all fall down.

Happy birthday, Ben. If he had any balls he'd have followed Frankie out the window. But no, not him. The baby broke and so did Ben and Maggie.

No more Frankie. No more Maggie.

Dr. Lambert shakes his head now. "I'm sorry. It must have been extremely painful to lose your child that way."

Got a little chart for pain there, Doctor? On a scale of one to blinding, where does *wrecked* fall?

Fistfuls of love one minute and the next it had all disintegrated—poured through Ben's fingers like sand.

Imagine the silence, the casket of a room once the police had left it, once the ambulance had taken Frankie's . . . and the neighbors had gone back inside, locking their locks behind them, locking out misery like a contagion.

Maggie and Ben: Now you see them; now you don't. The two of them lost in the smallest room in the world.

Maggie wouldn't go to work and she wouldn't pick up the phone. The old ladies kept calling. Ben would listen to their stuttering messages. There was no one to take them to their appointments or sweep their floors. "Maggie," they'd say, "I was late for my appointment . . . you were supposed to be here today at . . . I would appreciate it if . . . if you could at least . . ."

Message after message. Maggie never listened. She didn't speak.

At first Ben could feel her hovering, searching: for the baby—for Ben—but he couldn't—he couldn't face his own face, let alone hers.

Most days, Maggie would fill up the bathtub and lie in the water for hours at a time. Sometimes she would dress and drift out the door without a word. She would slip back into the apartment so quietly, Ben wouldn't know she was home until he heard the bathroom door close and the pipes groan as she filled the tub again.

And while Maggie filled the tub with water, Ben would fill a limo with gas and drive it around the city until dawn, long after his last ride of the night. He took every work call that came. One morning he got home, walked into the bathroom, and the mirror was gone. She'd taken it off the wall.

A couple of days later the mirror in the bedroom was gone too. And then the last one in the hall disappeared. Fine by him. Who wants to look in a glass and see his rotting soul reflected back?

Then he came home one morning and Maggie was gone. In a way, it was a perverse comfort to have the exterior match the interior. Empty/Empty.

She left a phone number. But he didn't phone it and it didn't phone him.

The old ladies kept phoning, though, looking for her. "Maggie, I have a doctor's appointment . . . Maggie, there's no tuna fish in the house . . . My library books are overdue . . . Maggie, Maggie, Maggie."

He listened to their messages when he should have been sleeping. He'd come home and listen. He'd sit there, watching the sun come up, listening to those goddamn messages, over and over, in case they changed, or he caught something he'd missed. With each listen, he despised them more—them and their dried-out spider plants, their dusty knick-knacks and expired coupons.

The one who called the most was the pill lady. Mrs. Riley and her Xanax, her Ambien, her Percocet—the bottles began to float in front of Ben's eyes like ghouls. Mrs. Riley's ugly minions.

After replaying one of her messages, Ben went into Maggie's address book and hunted for the pill lady. He watched his finger scrape down the page and land on the name. He picked up the phone and tapped out the number.

Her line rang and Ben stared into space, wondering. There was no purpose for this call. What could he possibly say to the woman? He should put down the phone, but it was as if he were paralyzed, as if his body belonged to someone else.

Then she picked up. "Hello?"

There was a long pause. She said hello again. And again. She asked if anyone was there.

Ben said, "Have I reached Mrs. Cecily G. Riley?" His voice was hollow and craggy, like a demon in the radio. "I'm calling about Maggie, your cleaning woman. Maggie won't be coming to work. I thought you might like to know why: Maggie's baby, Frankie, found a bottle of Xanax with the name Cecily G. Riley on it. He swallowed the pills and now he's dead."

At the other end of the line was a short, sharp little cry. And then Ben hung up.

He sat very still and waited and listened. He put his hand on his throat, feeling for a pulse. A part of him wondered if he was dead and if he was, then why the hell couldn't he lie down and be done with it.

TWO

Maggie

I fling through the lobby doors and hurl my purse at the pavement. *Fuck! WhatIsWrongWithMe? WhatIsWrongWithMe? WhatIsWrongWithMe, God Fucking Dammit, What Is* Wrong *With Me?* I can't be in the world anymore. I don't know how to be normal.

Construction continues to brawl and hammer across the road. I snatch my purse up off the ground, backhand the tears and snot off my face, and stare back at Lucy McVeigh's high-rise. So much for reentering the workforce. So much for becoming a stable human being again.

Across the road a dump truck is backing its way off the site. Backing and beeping. *Shut up!* All the traffic stops in both directions. The world stops for progress. Not for me, not for Frankie, just this goddamn building site.

I trudge toward the bus stop. The truck slowly moves forward, turning its nose north, and then roars up the hill, churning dust as it goes. A bus follows close on its heels, groaning to the inside lane. A bus? *My* bus. Shit. My bus.

Hugging my purse, I race for the bus stop, scrambling in hopes the driver might see me or hear me and take pity. "Wait. Hang on!" I trip and lose my shoe. And, of course, there is no pity.

"Oh, come on!" I pick my shoe up off the sidewalk and chuck it toward the exhaust that plumes from the back end of my ride home as it shrinks in the distance.

I limp the few feet to my shoe, and step into it.

A couple of teenage boys head in my direction, all torn jeans and lanky limbs, one tall with cautious, watchful eyes, the other small and grinning, snickering at me and my shoe.

I slump on the bench at the bus shelter.

As they pass, the small one loses interest in me. He casts his dreamy eyes at the bulldozers across the road, and then down at a bit of sunlit cellophane on the sidewalk. He picks it up: a discarded cigarette package. The taller boy bats it out of his hand.

"What the fuck, man!" the little one says. "There was still some smokes in it."

The tall one mumbles something and shoves him along. They remind me of Ben and Cola—Benjamin and Nicolas, but no one ever called them that. My Ben often called his little brother "Donkey Boy," after the Pinocchio story about boys who went to the Land of Toys—Pleasure Island—lured by the promise of fun, of never having to learn or work. As each one succumbed to his wayward desires he was transformed into a jackass. That little idiot is actually talented, Ben used to say. He talked about a chair that Cola made in high school: solid maple, polished, stained, perfect. It was art, Ben said. Cola gave it to his father for his birthday. It was barely a month before dear old Dad came home savage drunk and threw the chair in the street. A semitruck took care of the rest. Cola quit school and found work as a carpenter. Showed up drunk and got fired. Slept in and got fired. "Borrowed" a drill and got fired.

The Ben-size boy catches me watching, looks away, and gives the Cola boy another shove.

I look away too, down at my feet, and beyond them to the crack in the sidewalk: fall through the cracks, crack under pressure, hard nut to crack. I can hear Ben tying idioms into knots . . . the way his brain used to bob and weave. Now he's trying to weave his brain back together. I grab a last look at those Ben-and-Cola boys before they round the corner.

Who am I? Who am I without Ben? Who am I without Frankie? This is not how it was supposed to go. This is not who I thought I'd be at thirty-two years old. Something like a widow, but worse. What do you call the mother of a dead child? Besides negligent. Delinquent. Derelict.

I want to look after you. Ben said that. That was the plan. *I want to look after you.* In the middle of a night just after we moved in together, I woke in the dark: 3:34 A.M. Half an hour since the last time I'd woken up. I could feel the cool emptiness on Ben's side of the bed. Still at work. Closing my eyes again, I wished him close, imagined his limbs folding around me, the sensation of his breath on the back of my neck.

Then I heard breath. Actual breath. My eyes snapped open.

Ben stood at the foot of the bed. I gasped, startled.

"It's me—it's just me," he said.

"*Jesus!* What are you doing?" My heart hammered.

"Watching you sleep. You looked so sweet, lying there." He climbed up the length of the mattress, nestled in behind me, and put his arm around my waist. "Sorry. I didn't mean to scare you."

"I wasn't scared."

He brought his lips to my ear and murmured, "If I snored like you, I wouldn't be scared either."

"Shut up, I don't snore."

"You kidding? From out in the hall it sounded like a motorcycle gang in here. No burglar would chance it."

I laughed and elbowed him. "I do not snore." Taking a breath, I rolled onto my back and looked at him. "How was your night?"

"A stretch limo full of drunk dentists—couldn't have been better if they'd thrown in a free root canal. What about your day, Madam Moderator?"

At the time, I worked for a consumer research company. My job was to help facilitate focus groups. "We got another pep talk from the new analytics expert today. She's got a voice like a constipated goose: *'Desire is shaped by fear. The consumer desires a product when he fears what life might be like without it. It's your job to discover what that fear might be.'*"

Ben smirked. "Gandhi said that, didn't he?"

I ran a finger across his breast pocket. "Would you hate me if I quit?"

"Hate you?" He shook his head. "You said you wanted to quit the first time I met you, so . . ."

"But it's good money."

"But you're not happy."

My mouth opened and then closed. "The thing is—" I fidgeted with the button on his shirt collar. "I'm—I missed my period. I bought one of those tests today and it was . . . I'm—"

"Are you . . . ?"

I nodded.

He laid a hand against my cheek and blinked into my eyes. "Do you want this?"

Seconds passed. I couldn't speak. I didn't know what I wanted.

Ben watched me and swallowed. "I want this," he said. "Maggie, I—I've been waiting my whole life for you—for us. I want to look after you." He took a breath and rested his forehead against mine. "I love you. So much. Marry me. Just say yes, and I will cherish you, love you, and hold you until the day I die."

The sound of his voice: low and quiet and sure. He brought his face back from mine and there was just enough light to see the shine of his wet eyes. My throat seized. I felt like an orphaned kid all over again except this time the world was about to begin, not end.

"Yes." I could feel a sob building in my chest and I said yes again while I could still get the word out.

The rumble from across the road shakes me back into the bus shelter. Then I realize that my cell phone is vibrating. I find it at the bottom of my purse. "Holy Trinity" is on the call display. Francis. My brother is probably the only one I can bear this morning. So I put a finger in one ear and the phone up to the other.

"Hello, Maggie, it's Father Michael, the ah, the rector over at Holy Trinity. I'm calling about Luke." Luke is the religious name my brother took when he was ordained.

"What happened?"

There is a long pause and my stomach lurches.

"He's fine," the rector finally says. "I mean he's not hurt or anything, but we've had another situation. He was arrested night before last. Another DUI."

"Sonuvabitch!"

Father Michael gives a nervous laugh. "Ah, well, yes, he's not handling it very well. He's locked himself, ah, he won't come out of his room. He—"

"I thought you said he was in jail."

"He was. For a few hours. We brought him back here. And, as I say, he's not doing very well. We wondered if it might be better if he stayed with family for a few days until this blows over."

"Until what blows over?"

"Ah, well, maybe it's better if I let your brother explain. Maggie, I'm sorry, but you're the only family he has. We understand you've been—it's been terrible for you lately, and we think that for this very reason, it'd be a good idea for Luke to be with you."

Father Michael tells me to take a cab. He'll pay, he says.

FINE, YOU PAY. You pay and you deal with him. You people wanted him, body and soul, so you deal with him, body and soul.

That's what I should have said. But instead, I sit here in the back of a taxi that is hauling my butt down to Holy Trinity because my idiot brother is stuck in his holy-man room with his head up his ass. Barely heard a word from him since the funeral. I have been—my child is—his nephew, his namesake—and Francis is busy getting his wild on. There is real shit going on in this world with real consequences, but no, it's all about Francis and his little pity party. I'd like to kick his self-absorbed ass up one side of that rectory and down the other.

As we near Holy Trinity, it's as if the circus has come to town. News vans are parked out front, there are people milling on the sidewalk, creeping up the church lawn, sitting on the steps. A couple of men in suits are holding microphones and pacing, looking up at the church doors in case something should haul off and happen. Fox News, local news, *Good Morning America*, even.

The cabdriver slows and then I see chubby little Father Michael on the corner, standing there in his clerics, shaking his head, no, at a couple of scrappy-looking reporters who push recorders in his face. His palms are cupped together in front of his belly as if he's Mother Superior instead of the squirmy little worm that he is.

Seeing the cab, he scurries into the street and pushes his puffy red face in the driver's-side window. While he pays, I get out and gawp at the sight of all the trucks with satellite dishes sitting in front of the church.

The taxi clears off and Father Michael takes my arm as if I'm a geriatric.

"What the hell is going on?" I ask. Wordlessly, he hustles me toward the side entrance. I look over my shoulder at the mess of them. "Did they find another pedophile or something?"

Father Michael closes the door behind us and faces me with a petulant scowl. "No."

The relative quiet settles over us. I look behind him down the hall that leads to the actual church. Upstairs is the seminary, the dormitory that houses a mix of priests and students. I haven't been here in eight or nine years, but the smell of the place, the institutional scent of books and floor wax, mixed with rose-scented incense, raises my hackles instantly.

"Maggie," he says, "we're all really worried about him, about Father Luke, ah, your Francis. That video they took is all over the place and those newspeople have been here since six this morning. We can't—I mean, you're his sister."

"What video? I have no idea what's been going on around here. So you'll have to enlighten me."

Father Michael takes a breath and collects himself. "He was arrested the night before last. The police videotaped his time in the holding cell and then somebody down there put out this thing, this—misleading!—version of what happened. You know, because if you were to look at it—"

"Where is he?"

"Room 309. On the third floor. Thank you, Maggie. This will mean so much to him."

I STEP OFF the elevator into a hurricane of music pounding down the hall. Not a hymn, but club music with crashing techno drums and a wailing bass guitar. I suppose that's him.

Oh, for God's sake. What is he, sixteen?

I stalk off toward the hell-voice of Marilyn Manson growling about being a personal Jesus.

The lyrics and their promise of someone to hear your prayers, someone who cares, Manson's roaring command to reach out and touch faith, sends an involuntary shudder down my spine. The song ends abruptly and two seconds later, it's back to the beginning, thundering into the air once more.

I hammer his door with my fist. "Francis! Open up. Right now." I can hear myself channeling our mother and that's not helping. Or maybe it is. "Francis! I mean it. Turn that shit off and open the door."

I give the knob a try and it turns. The door opens slowly. Now the music is truly head-pounding.

His single bed is crisply made, but I don't see my brother anywhere. I see only where he lives and I turn in a slow circle, looking into the faces of countless saints. Nearly every inch of all four walls is covered with small wooden plaques, painted in golds and ambers, each one depicting a sacred event or a holy person. For years now, a tiny part of me has wondered if this priest stuff is just an escape for Francis, a costume he is trying on—like a Batman suit for Catholics. Now, staring at the doting eyes in icon after icon, it occurs to me that the man who sleeps here craves salvation the way some crave food or sex.

I walk over to his stereo and just as I am about to push the power button, I see my brother on the far side of his bed, prostrate, face to the floor, wearing his cassock. Laid out in front of him is a purple cloth embossed with a gold cross. On it I recognize the small figure of St. Francis of Assisi that he's had since we were kids. It is flanked by candles that cast low, toothy shadows on the bedspread and the wall. Beside St. Francis is another saint I don't recognize. Luke, maybe?

I kill the power on the stereo. The sudden silence is like static on the air.

My brother's head rises so slowly that I am suddenly a little afraid for him. His eyes are red and swollen, and tears track down his cheeks. On the floor in the spot where his forehead had rested is a photograph. It is a picture of a little boy in his puffy snowsuit, knee-deep in fresh powder, grinning and pink-cheeked. My Frankie.

Quiet crackles in my ears. My eyes sting. My guts hurt.

I come closer. Kneeling beside him, I lay my arm across my brother's back, whisper that I'm here. It's okay.

IT's NOT DIFFICULT to persuade Francis to come with me. He packs silently and as he does, I glance around at his walls again. Nobody craves this kind of company without reason.

Even the thirteen-inch television that sits on his bureau has a Madonna and child icon set on top. The baby looks like a tiny, knowing man standing in her arms. One of his hands caresses her jaw.

Francis zips his bag, we turn out the light, close the door behind us, and head down to the underground parking. We don't stop to talk to the rector.

My brother hands me his keys and I drive his green rust bucket out the back of the church property and over to my place.

A HALF HOUR later, we are sitting on my couch, drinking tea and making stilted conversation.

"I love these old heritage houses," Francis says. "How many apartments in here?"

"Five."

His long black eyelashes flutter about the room. "Is this all their furniture?"

I nod. Even in the midst of this mess, my brother's hair is combed and lacquered in place; his shirt crisp, and clean.

"The rent is pretty cheap. And I don't have to share a bathroom, which is a relief."

"Right, right. It looks nice, sweetheart." He nods. I nod. He looks toward the window. "Are you working these days?"

I shake my head. "I went for an interview this morning. It was going great until I started bawling. It's—Frankie comes into my head. And this stuff with Ben—I just, I feel like a stupid, useless walking sore."

Francis looks down into his mug for two or three long seconds. "Have you heard from Ben? From the hospital?"

"No. They called when he came out of surgery last week. It's amazing that he's okay. Who survives that? Well, I guess he survived. He's in a psych ward now."

My brother meets my eye for the first time since we got here. "I feel like maybe I should go down and see him."

My mouth opens. I don't know quite what to say to that.

He sighs. "I know. But I'm still a priest. He's clearly been going through a spiritual crisis of some kind. You both have. Have you—"

"Physician, heal thyself," I mutter.

He snorts softly and looks into his mug again. After a while he says, "I know it bugged you when I took a religious name. Hardly anyone does it anymore. I picked St. Luke because he's known as the Divine Physician. I thought that when I took his name, somehow it might be healing. So . . . so much for that."

I watch him and chew at my bottom lip.

Francis pulls a pack of cigarettes out of his pocket. He lights one and puffs and then leans forward, elbows on his knees. "Have you seen this fucking video or what?"

"No. I didn't know anything about it until your rector called me. What's the big deal? A million drunks on YouTube, and yours goes viral? What makes you so damn special?"

"Well . . ." He smirks and bats his eyes. Almost like normal. Almost like we're "us" again.

"Seriously, are you totally annihilated? Have you got your pecker out or something?"

"No! I had a drink with a couple friends. I actually went home early. And I wasn't even driving when the cops pulled up. Next thing I know, the headlines are all screaming: DRUNK PRIEST! Whoop-de-doo."

"I'm sorry they did this to you, Francis."

His face softens and his eyes glass up a bit as if he might cry. He reaches for my hand and gives it a squeeze.

"What happens now?"

He stares at his cigarette for a moment. "They have me booked for six months in Our Lady of Perpetual Help Rehab Center. Father Michael and the parish lawyer are trying to get the court date set for after my rehab. Of course the court might refuse. This is my third DUI."

His third DUI. I look at Francis. His eyes flick from his cigarette to the floor. He reaches for his mug, I do the same, and the two of us sit there quietly sipping.

Ben

"Why don't we pick up where we left off yesterday," Dr.
Lambert says.

Yesterday? Used to be an old Jamaican lady who ran the
corner store when we were kids. She'd say, *A thousand years
in God's sight are like yesterday—already past—like a watch in the
night.* My old man would bitch all the way home, *Christ, I aged
about fifty just waitin' for my change.*

What do you think that means, *a watch in the night?*

"It's one of the Psalms, isn't it?" Lambert says. "I think it
refers to a shepherd's watch . . . night watch, a watch in the
night."

Shepherd's watch. Some shepherd. A watch in the night
is like a thousand years in Ben's soul. Like a thousand white
rooms. A thousand bullets to the brain.

"Sounds like your father continues to make quite an im-
pression," Lambert says.

At least he kept his kids from falling out open windows.

"Were you able to turn to your father for support after your son's death?"

Ben turned to his father, sure. Gotta try, right? The old man sounded like he was going to cry when he got the news. "No!" he said. "How? What the hell was going on? Were you drunk? Were you passed out?" Then he told Ben about the time he fell off a roof. He could've been killed.

Few days later, Ben tried again. Called him about the funeral. "A funeral," the old man said, sounding half-crocked. "A funeral? You think that poor little bugger woulda liked sittin' in a pew listening to all that gloomy shit? No way."

He told him that Maggie's brother, Francis, was going to say the mass.

"Father Fruit?" he said. "Bad enough she had to name my grandson after that one, now he's getting in on this? When I was a kid, priests were men, not like nowadays. When my mother died, they didn't bring me to any damn funeral. You know what they said to me?"

"Right. You can't make it," Ben said. "Gotta go." He tried to end the call but he kept hitting the wrong button on the handset. After a while he smashed the receiver against the coffee table until dear old Dad finally shut the fuck up.

The old man says he doesn't drink anymore. Claims he's been sober ten years. Sober's not quite the word. He still swallows anything that gets him high. Anything but booze. He loves his tranquilizers. And if the quacks won't give him junk, he'll make do with cough syrup.

One night he called Ben's cell phone. It was one in the morning and Ben had a party in the back of a stretch limo:

four hedge fund managers, four hookers. All of them loaded, wailing out the windows, out the moonroof.

Ben saw the caller ID. It was not a good time. He checked the rearview, the side mirrors, trying to make sure none of those assholes in the back got his head sideswiped by a truck.

The phone stopped buzzing. And started up again. Hadn't heard from him in weeks and now he was going to keep calling till Ben picked up. And don't kid yourself, Ben had to pick up. His old man was seventy-five now.

So Ben hit the Bluetooth. "Dad, I'm at work. Anything wrong?"

"How y'doin', kid? S'your old man."

"Yup. I'm working. Is it important?"

"Can't I call up my own son for chrissake?" Ben heard him trip over something and curse. "I can't sleep," he said. "I went to renew my pills yesterday and that bitch wouldn't give 'em to me. What the hell's happened to this goddamn country? It's just Xanax."

Ben's guts turned into a fist at the mention of Xanax. It was barely a month since Frankie died. "You sound pretty wasted as it is."

"Bullshit. I'm sober as a fuckin' judge. I tried to get something off whatshername, that fat broad next door. Now she's not answering. Can you gimme something?"

"I don't have anything."

"Don't bullshit a bullshitter. All those rich people you drive around, they must have all kinds of good stuff on 'em."

Behind Ben's head, the car's blackout partition rolled down and the sound of thumping club music invaded the driver's seat.

One of the hedge fund managers staggered on his knees to the spot behind Ben. "You wanna get in on this?" He put his arm through the window and offered a palm full of coke. "Got a lotta pussy back here." His nose and upper lips were dusted in white powder. His tongue flicked and he smacked his lips.

Ben looked in the rearview mirror: a woman was holding the edge of the moonroof as she gyrated, her clothes being removed by one of the men. Kitty-corner to her, a second woman, wearing nothing but silver platform shoes, held the opposite edge of the moonroof as a second man knelt and lapped at her crotch.

Deep in the back, it was a tangle of tongues and holes and limbs.

"What's going on there?" the old man said. "You at a god-damn party or what? You talked to your brother? Damn kid needs an attitude adjustment. If he doesn't straighten out, he's going to land himself in jail and I'm sure as hell—"

"I gotta go." Ben hung up. In his side mirror, cop lights flashed blue and red.

He was about to pull over, but the patrol car flew up the outside lane and disappeared around the next corner. He glanced over his shoulder at the man with the coke. "No thanks," he said. "Looks like you guys got it covered."

"Sure?" The guy put his empty hand on Ben's shoulder, gave it a little squeeze. "Come on, man."

"Keep up the good work," Ben told him. The guy backed off and Ben rolled the partition up. He drove toward the water.

At the end of the night, he dropped all eight of them out

front of the Grand Marquis. Sitting in the car under the hotel portico, he watched them traipse into the lobby. He looked at the uniformed doormen, the bellhops and valets, and wondered what the likelihood was that any of them would turn down free coke. Or pussy.

He glanced at his reflection, the bloodshot eyes, the bruise-colored bags. Can't sleep? Join the club. He picked up his phone, checked the recent calls. No one.

They tipped him two hundred tonight. He'll give Maggie half. He'll call her and tell her about this fucked-up ride and the coke and the guy's hand on his shoulder. He'll ask how she's making out and offer to stop by.

The phone buzzed. Cola.

Ben hit the Bluetooth. "Hey, man."

"*As-salamu alaykum*, my brotha. You workin'?"

"Just dropped 'em off. You talk to the old man lately?"

"Are you kidding? He calls me every day. *Tell your old man something nice. Something from when you were a kid. I didn't do so bad with you boys, did I?*"

Ben paused. He couldn't tell if Cola was bragging or complaining.

"He sure was Robo-trippin' tonight." Cola meant the old man'd been chugging Robitussin DM again. "Hey, wanna meet me at Denny's? I could go for a Grand Slam."

So there's Ben at the end of another shitty Saturday night, sitting in the window booth at Denny's, mouth full of pancake and gloom. Been an hour since he heard from his brother and he's too tired to wait much longer. Going on five in the morning, but nobody in here's been to bed yet.

Finally he sees Cola coming up the sidewalk, skinny and

pale under the streetlights. His brother shoulders his way through the diner's front doors and stands there, squinting under fluorescence. He swipes his hair back. It's always hanging in his eyes like a kid's.

Cola spots Ben in the window booth, shakes his head no, and heads to a table farther in.

After a minute or so, Ben hears, *"Psst."* He's too tired for punk brother shit right now. So he just sits and looks out the window, watches a couple of the night's last stragglers stumble against the dark windows of his curbside limo and then knock on the glass before they wander off.

From over his shoulder, another *"Psst. Ben!"*

He can feel Cola wiggling in his seat the way he did when they were kids. He pictures that diner they stopped at off the highway. Twenty-five years ago. He was ten and Cola six. The old man had finished his second beer and had gone to take a leak when the waitress set three plates on the table. House rules: no eating without Dad. Dad took forever. Probably had a bottle in there, busy making his beers into boilermakers.

Cola got fizzy with waiting. Quit screwing around, Ben told him. But he didn't make him stop.

Tongue between his teeth, Cola picked up his plate of spaghetti and balanced it on the point of his knife. He gave the plate a spin and wound up with the whole writhing mess all over the table, the floor, and himself.

The old man hauled Ben outside. "That's my money he was dumping on his head! Little shit-for-brains—you just sit there?" Slap in the mouth.

No saving face. The face is the first to know.

That was then. Here's Ben and Cola in a whole other

diner, twenty-five years later, and nothing's changed much. A whistle shoots from the space between Cola's front teeth until Ben finally looks over. Cola coaxes him with a jerk of his head.

Ben watches a waitress pause to fill Cola's cup. Cola looks at the jut of her hip. She's young enough that even stiff brown polyester looks half-decent. She's lingering for an excuse to push that flop of hair out of Cola's eyes, take him home and keep him for a pet. Forget it, girlie, Cola's too busy trying to spin plates.

Ben wipes his mouth, picks up his jacket, and schleps to his brother's booth.

"Why'd you sit at a window?" Cola says. "I can't be all exposed like that."

"*Exposed?* Who're you, Al Capone?" Ben takes a seat. "You must owe someone a real chunk of change this time."

"I'll pay 'em back next week." He sets his tongue between his teeth as he dumps sugar into his coffee.

Ben shrugs. "Tell them to get in line."

"It's no joke. Dudes were waiting outside my place last night. Had to stay at Vera's. Man, you look like shit, brother. You still not sleeping?"

"How much are you into them for?"

"Eight grand."

Ben stares.

"It was a sure thing. OxyContin. Buddy had a shitload of it." Off Ben's confused face, he murmurs, "It's like morphine."

"I know what it is." Ben blinks, waiting. "What are you playing at this crap for? I thought you had a construction gig."

"That shit's for suckers."

"They fired your ass."

"You wanna hear this or not? Oxy's huge, man—hillbilly heroin! It's bigger than meth, coke, everything. There's places down south where all anyone does is score oxy. So, check this: Buddy sells to me for ten bucks a tab, and then I move it at fifty, sixty a tab. I'd be sitting on forty grand now." His eyes flit across the restaurant. "I borrowed the money and fronted the guy eight grand. Now I can't find him."

"You *fronted* him the money? This is a whole new level of stupid."

"No way, man. We were going to be partners—he had the connection for the stuff and I had a connection for the money. This guy is solid. He must've got busted."

"How long since you saw him?"

"Two weeks. S'okay, I got another plan."

"To prey on a bunch of addicts?"

Cola laughs. "Hypocrite. Just 'cause you never had the balls to think big."

Ben nods at the table. "You're right—I'm the asshole," he mutters. "Barely pay my rent. Can't look after Maggie."

"Maggie? Why you gotta look after her? Not like she needs—" Cola stops. He looks at Ben. "I mean she's alone. It's not like—"

Ben's jaw works as he pulls out his wallet. "I gotta go." He slides out a ten-dollar bill. "Oh wait, you're broke, right?" Cola is silent. Ben shoves the ten back and chucks a twenty on the table.

"Come on, don't get all pissed. I got a plan. This time next week, we'll be cool. Hey, what'd the old man say tonight?

Did he tell you he keeps puking? He told me not to tell you. And his stomach's sticking out like there's a football in there. That cough syrup shit, man, he'd be better off with booze. I'm starting to think we should put him in a home or something."

"They should put *me* in a home." Ben stands. "I got to get the car back."

"All right. Get some sleep, brother. Seriously."

"Get a job." Ben heads for the door.

"Hey, Ben! Don't tell the old man, okay? About the eight grand. Okay?"

Maggie

Francis taps on my bedroom door at ten in the morning. "Are you awake?"

"Entrez."

He opens the door and stands there lit from behind. "Did I wake you?"

"Nope." I've actually been awake a half hour or so, staring into the dark of my windowless bedroom.

"It kills me in here," he says with a laugh. "That tiny little bed—it's like a monk's cell."

I turn on the lamp, prop myself up on my elbows, and look at him in his royal blue pajamas with the white piping. He's wearing cotton espadrilles and his hair is combed into place.

"What?" he says. "What are you looking at?"

"Drunk Priest Propositions Cops."

"Oh. That."

"Yeah, *that*. Imagine my surprise to see my dear brother,

the YouTube sensation, chained to the wall of a drunk tank, saying, *I'll give you the Sermon on the Mount. Your Sermon on the Mount is this: Get these fucking cuffs off me, cuz they're giving me a rash!"*

Francis groans. He takes two steps in and sits on my bed.

"You left a bit out when you were filling me in," I say.

"Yeah, but, Maggie, they make it sound like I'd been partying all night. I was with a couple of friends. I had one lousy drink."

"Really?" I reach over the side of my bed and pick up my laptop.

"Don't."

I click play and there's Francis wearing chocolate-colored trousers, a tartan vest, and bright orange socks. He tugs at the handcuff attached to a bolt in the white wall of the cell, sways in the direction of the camera, and demands to be released. Then he tries begging. "Please. I'm not an animal. Let me go. I'll do whatever you want. Want me to suck you off? Is that what you—"

Francis slaps my laptop closed. "I didn't proposition them."

"I know. I watched the short 'n' sneaky edit first. Then I watched the uncut version where you refuse to be a sexual slave. I like the part where you sing 'Freedom.' You actually do a pretty good George Michael."

"Shut it, okay." He picks at a cigarette burn on his otherwise dapper pajama pants.

"Me shut it? You shut it. You blew three times the legal limit!"

"I did not. I don't know where they're getting their—"

"Right, cuz you don't look shitfaced at all. It was a setup."

"Everything isn't always how it looks." He pulls a pack of smokes from his pocket.

"It isn't? Well, that's a relief because it looked like you were wearing neon orange socks. Were you out rabbit hunting that day, Father Fudd?"

He snorts, closes his eyes tight, and opens them. "Maybe this could be my audition reel for *Celebrity Rehab with Dr. Drew*: me and Janice Dickinson." He pulls out a cigarette and flicks his lighter, then pauses and looks at me. "May I?"

"I'd tell you to piss off, but I'm brimming with sympathy this morning."

He takes a long drag, and slaps his lighter and cigarette package down on the bed.

I rest my head against the wall and watch him smoke for a few moments. "Have you got a lawyer?"

Francis nods, opens his mouth, and the thick cloud of smoke released seems to circle his head like a halo. "He called this morning. He thinks he's going to have to double his fee."

"That's what he called to tell you? He's doubling his fee?"

"Yup. Because the video's gone viral. He says it's done terrible damage to me and therefore he's in a better position to do some damage to the police. It's a bigger case than he thought, and *much* more complicated. Asshole."

I watch the ash build on the end of his cigarette and hand him an empty mug from my nightstand. "What's going on with you?"

"I told you. They've put me on leave. Rehab starts in a week. Hopefully."

I stare at him.

He taps ash into the mug and lies back across the bottom of my narrow bed, head and shoulders against the wall. "I don't know."

I nudge him with my foot. "Yeah, you do. Your *third* DUI?"

He takes another long drag, blows it to the ceiling, and blinks at the drifting smoke. "I like it here. The phone doesn't ring." He turns his head to me.

"I know what you mean." I pluck the cigarette out of his hand and take a puff. My first since I found out I was pregnant with Frankie.

"Lately," he says, "it's like I feel all this anxiety when I have to be around people. When I go out anywhere—even at the church." He takes his cigarette back and examines it a moment. "Especially at the church. It's gotten so bad I'm scared to go downstairs after the liturgy. We always have a little snack and coffee after the service. But these days I run into the rectory and hide. I'm scared when the phone rings; email makes me feel as if someone is in my room."

"You went through something like this when you first went into the seminary. They said you were agoraphobic."

He does an imitation of me. *"Does that mean you're afraid to wear fuzzy sweaters?"*

"Sorry. Maybe you're just not—maybe the church isn't the right place for you."

"Here we go." Francis sits up. "You think you're helping when you start this, but you're not." He gets up off the bed, and holding his cigarette over the mug, he drifts out to the living room.

"Yeah, here we go again," I call through the door. "I hit a nerve and you fuck off. You know, I'm only—" My cell phone

buzzes. I pick it up off the nightstand. The number's familiar. Answer it? Don't answer it? "Hello?"

"Have I reached Maggie? It's Lucy McVeigh from the other
day. Yesterday."

My chest seizes. Here we go, here we go, wherever you go,
it's here we go.

"Oh, yes. Hi, Lucy. Ah, I'm very sorry for how our meeting
ended yesterday. I'm, I guess I—"

"Me too. I've been thinking about you and it seems to me
that it would be a good thing for us to do a trial run."

My brother stands in the middle of the living room, smoking and peering in at me. "Who is it?" he mouths.

"You seem like a good person," Lucy says. "I think we
should try each other out."

Repeating her words in my head, I search for my own. "Are
you, ah, I'm not sure if I've—"

"Your ad said you have a driver's license. I've got a car, but
I've got macular degeneration, so I can't see so hot."

The way my heart is pounding, you'd think someone was
trying to break through the front door. My brother watches
with questioning bug-eyes. Maybe there is something geneti-
cally wrong with Francis and me.

My mouth has gone dry. "When would you need me?"

"Tonight. Could you be here at six thirty? I'll pay you for
four hours."

Tonight? I can't go somewhere tonight. What am I going
to say to this woman for four hours? It feels like I'm going to
cry again.

"Twenty bucks an hour," she says. "Yes or no?"

I can't. I can't do anything for four hours. *What is wrong with you? It's four hours, not four days. What do you want to do, go live in a cave? Move to the psych ward with Ben?* "Okay. Ah, I will be there. Six thirty. Can I ask where we'll be going—do I need to be concerned with attire?"

"Wear whatever you'd wear to church."

Great.

FOUR

Ben

Ben drives around the city till the sun comes up before he brings the limo back. At six thirty in the morning, he idles in front of Maggie's place, a big old Victorian manor, chopped into bite-size pieces. He goes into his pocket, takes his paycheck out of its envelope, and stuffs in the hedge funders' two hundred. He prints "Maggie" on the envelope. He stares at her name. What else is there to say? "I thought you could use this." No. He turns the envelope over. "I hope you are okay." Ben? Love, Ben? He used to write "Your Ben" with X's and O's. Plain Ben is all there is now.

Out of the car, he heads for the mailboxes grouped near the walkway. He finds Maggie's name, her Suite 5 slot. He smooths the envelope, folds it, and jams it through the opening. He picks off the bits of paper that tear free and cling to the thin metal mouth. Then he glances at the big old house and dashes back to the limo as if the front door might open. As if there might be consequences.

They say you can't go home again, but the truth is, you have to. You have to sit still in your godforsaken living room and watch gold sunlight coming through the blinds. You have to hear the tweeting birds and the coughing crows and face the fact that no one else is coming through the front door.

He gave up on the bedroom weeks ago—too little sleep and too many dreams of Maggie breathing next to him. He could feel the weight of her there, the dip in the mattress, and then he'd open his eyes to nothing but nothingness. Now he stays on the couch where he knows what's what. Here there is only room for Ben. Sometimes he even drifts off for an hour or so. This morning it might have been two hours that he was lost in dark limbo before his phone buzzed him awake.

It's Cola calling from Vera's place. "Hey, man, did I wake you?"

Ben squints at his watch. Ten o'clock. "What do you want?"

"I talked to the old man after I saw you. He sounded really fucked-up."

"Yeah."

"I'm serious. I started thinking if he went to sleep, he might not wake up. Like, maybe I should call an ambulance. But then I thought, if he's okay, he'll be really pissed with me calling an ambulance. I phoned him back and it was busy."

"He's probably sleeping it off."

"I called again this morning and it's still busy."

"What do you want?"

"Maybe we should—I don't know. Vera says—"

"What the fuck, Cola? What are you so inside out about? He does this. He trips over the phone and doesn't hang it up."

Cola mumbles and mutters. In the background, his girl-friend, Vera, suggests and proposes.

"I'll talk to you later," Ben says and puts the phone down. He sits up and checks his calls. Nothing else since last night: just Cola and dear old Dad.

What day is today? Did she check her mailbox yet? Maybe Ben should call and let her know. He picks up his cell phone, finds her number, and hovers his thumb over the keypad. Don't do it. She doesn't want to talk to you.

He lies back on the couch, stares at the ceiling until his eyes sting. He closes them, and then he's hit with a wave of claustrophobia so bad he's got to sit up to breathe.

In the kitchen, he puts coffee on and leans against the counter. Cola's hand-wringing words loiter in his head: "Don't tell the old man, okay? About the eight grand. Okay?" Juxtapose that with "He calls me every day."

The old man calls Cola every day, and phones Ben every few weeks.

Could be worse, could be the other way around.

Ben picks up his phone, dials his father. Busy. He tries again. Busy. He looks at his watch. Sticking his phone in his back pocket, he goes into the fridge, grabs the bread and the package of smoked ham beside it.

He stands over the sink, eats a dry slice with a slab of meat, and thinks about whether there's any point in going over there. Cola talks to him every day, but thinks it's Ben who should drop by and make sure everything's copacetic.

He takes a swig of bitter coffee.

His ass vibrates and Ben takes the phone out of his

pocket: Cola again, calling from his cell this time. Ben stuffs that last bit of food in his mouth and guzzles the rest of his coffee. "Yup."

"We're at his door. He's not answering. My key doesn't work. You got a key, too, right? What if he's in a coma? Vera thinks we should bust in."

"Chrissake," Ben says.

Twenty minutes later, Ben's key is opening the door to the old man's apartment, Cola and his girl at his shoulder.

As the door opens, the stench hits. Ben reaches inside and flips the light switch. Nothing.

"Dad?" He steps into the room. That's all it is, a one-room studio with too much furniture. Ben squints in the darkness. Shots of light sneak through tears in the blackout drapes: overturned chairs, busted mirror, busted radio, busted glasses. Scattered pills and cassette tapes, half-eaten tins of tuna and sardines.

Ben runs the obstacle course around the corner of the L-shaped room to the bed. Nothing but a rumple of stinking sheets and blankets. "He's not here."

"What?" Cola comes up behind Ben. "He never goes anywhere."

Ben yanks open the tattered blackout drapes. The balcony is piled high with stuffed green trash bags. He slides open the door to let in some air.

Now he can see the filthy walls, the slice of pizza ground into the rug, tortilla chips, brown splotches on the sheets dappled with sticky green, a couple of empty cough syrup bottles on the nightstand, more trash bags against the walls.

"This is a health hazard," Vera says. "Your dad should be in a facility."

Cola's new girlfriend, Vera, is a veterinary technician. Small and wiry and insistent: Ben sees a Jack Russell terrier whenever he looks at her.

Stepping backward, Ben stumbles: A sardine tin tips onto his shoe, fish and oil dripping. Jesus Christ. He kicks it off.

From the bathroom, Vera says, "Oh my fucking God," and flushes the toilet.

"Last night he said some guy down the hall had some apples for him," Cola says. "There's demented people in here, man. It's a seniors building!"

"We should go door-to-door," Vera says and scurries out into the hall. Cola chases after her and stands behind her as she raps on the first door. No answer.

Ben takes out his phone, searches for the nearest hospital, and dials.

Vera rushes to the next apartment. The door opens and she barks the old man's name, demands to know his where-abouts.

"Who are you?" a small voice answers.

Ben sticks a finger in his ear as he is put through to Emergency. They've got him. The old man was brought in by ambulance. Ben asks if he overdosed.

"We can't give that information over the phone. Are you family?"

"I just told you, I'm his son," Ben says. "Are you a nurse? Can I talk to someone who knows something?" Again she says they can't give out any more information over the phone.

Ben hangs up and shouts, "He's in the emergency room!"

Cola and Vera stand in the door. Cola's pupils are large and black and darting.

"The people in this building are very rude," Vera says.

BEN WALKS INTO Emergency, Cola and Vera trailing. He stops beside the nurse's station and turns around, looking bed to bed, wherever curtains are open. His eyes pause over a scrawny old man, legs almost hairless, his thin flesh sagging off the bone. His forehead seems bulbous over his tiny pointed chin and it makes him look more creature than human.

An involuntary shudder quakes through Ben as recognition sets in. He walks closer. His old man couldn't weigh more than a hundred and twenty pounds. When did he last see him? Two months ago? Three?

Lying on his side, kicking at the sheets, pawing the air, he looks as if he's trying to climb the hospital bed, up the wall to escape. His gown is open at the back. He's wearing a thick white diaper.

The bedside machine sounds off with loud fast beeps until someone in green scrubs moves in. "Lie back, Mr. Brody." The nurse picks the heart sensor off the bed and reattaches it to the old man's finger. "Mr. Brody, lie down—you're going to pull out your IV."

"Dad?"

The old man blinks for a moment, lips sunken against his gums. No dentures. "Hey, you're here. Look at that, my sons." He smiles gappily. His focus floats around the room.

Cola goes to the foot of the bed. "Hey, Dad."

Ben turns to the guy in scrubs. "What's going on?"

Turns out, there's a twist in his old man's colon. He's going to need a section removed once they get his platelets up. The nurse asks if he's on any blood thinners.

Ben shakes his head. "All kinds of sedatives—Lunesta, Xanax, Ambien, Ativan, whatever he can get hold of. I don't know what all's in his system right now."

"He drinks cough syrup. Anything with dextromethorphan," Vera blurts.

"If there's acetylsalicylic acid in the kind he drinks, that might be lowering his platelet count."

"What?" the old man shouts, his shriveled lips caught between a sneer and a pout. "What are you whispering about?"

Cola puts his arm around Vera as though she is his blankie.

VERA DRIVES BEN back to his car, her hands at precisely ten and two on the steering wheel. Riding shotgun, Cola gulps down her every word.

"Seriously," she says, "you two need to move your father into a facility. The fact that he was able to hide what was going on—he could have died. If it were my father—" Nip nip nip, snap snap snap.

The old fucker should be in a facility all right, the kind with bars on the windows and three squares.

EIGHT THAT EVENING, Ben is on the couch brooding at the ceiling of his apartment. *You two need to move your father into a facility.*

"You two" means "one Ben." It means that if Ben gave a shit he'd get a second job, he'd get a third. If Ben were any kind of man he'd take up bank robbery or pimping and get his father into a facility.

Veterinary technicians make good coin, don't they? Why doesn't Vera fork over five grand a month if she's so fired up about facilities?

His mind has just driven headlong into *And what the hell is a know-it-all like Vera doing with a fuckup like Cola?* when his phone rings. It's the hospital. The old man has gone into surgery.

Immediately after Ben hangs up, Cola calls. He tells Ben that at Critter Care Veterinary, where Vera works, a twelve-year-old schnauzer had the same colon surgery and the dog came through with flying colors. "Dog's older than Dad in dog years." There's a long pause. Then Cola's voice gets small and pleading. "Ben, what if this is it?"

What if? Damn well should be it. If the universe were just. If there were a God, the old man would've fallen out a window and not Ben's kid. Then again, who knows: If the old man won't come to the window, maybe the window will come to the old man.

THREE HOURS LATER, Ben's eyelids have dropped. He is knocking at the door to sleep when the phone jangles him awake. Midnight.

Hospital calling. The old man is in recovery. He should heal nicely, the surgeon says. There won't be any need for a colostomy bag.

Bully for him. Ben hangs up.

He paces the living room. At the window he looks down.

Staring at the pavement below, he opens his cell phone and dials.

He listens to her number ring. Goose bumps prick as though he's been splashed with ice water.

Answer. Come on, answer!

When she finally does, a little jolt shoots through his limbs. His voice slides in his throat like warm, golden honey. "Is that Mrs. Cecily G. Riley? Hello, Mrs. Riley. I'm calling about your prescriptions. Mrs. Riley, are you aware that Xanax is a controlled substance? It's illegal for you to give your prescribed pills to another person. And you did that, didn't you, Mrs. Riley? You gave away dozens. *Hundreds*."

"Why? Why are you doing this? What—" Her words catch and stumble.

Ben pictures her sitting in an armchair, one gnarled hand trembling over her eyes in fear and grief. Holding the receiver to his ear, he feels, for a moment, as if someone has cut the noose around his neck, as if he can breathe again. He hangs up.

FOUR

Maggie

We aren't in the car thirty seconds before Lucy starts in with the questions. "Do you go to church?" "What about when you were a little girl?" "What religion are you?" "My Lloyd used to call himself a recovering Catholic. Do you believe all that stuff about the virgin birth?" "What self-respecting woman could stand being in the Catholic Church?"

I haven't driven a car much lately. It's dark and rainy and I don't need an interrogation. Especially while driving someone else's fat old box of a Volvo. I turn the tables. "So how did you become a children's writer?"

"Oh!" Her tone changes to one of delight. "I used to be a doctor's receptionist, which I never enjoyed. Retiring was even worse. Then Lloyd said to me, 'Why don't you write more of those kids' poems?' When Lloyd's niece was a little girl, I wrote her a story-poem about a duck and an alligator. Dori Duck and Arty Alligator. She loved it."

"Mmhmm." I squint ahead at the glittering wet street.

"He bought me one of those children's writing market books. Since then, I've had over a hundred poems published in children's magazines—*Turtle Diary, Chipper, Alley-Oop*—all thanks to Lloyd. I thought some of my long poems could make a nice picture book, so I started sending to publishers. I was turned down by forty-six publishing houses! Some of them complained that they didn't like *anthropomorphism*." Lucy huffs in disbelief. "Kids *love* talking animals! Anyway, finally I sent a manuscript to FlyHigh Press in California and I got a contract! Did I tell you that *Pennywhistle* won a silver medal in the Strawberry Shortcake Awards? As of this year, it's sold almost twenty-eight thousand copies!"

"Wow! That's terrific."

"I wrote a second one called *Pennywhistle Flies,* but it didn't do as well. Here it is—this is us on the right."

We pull into the parking lot at five to seven. The place appears to be a former residence: someone's white clapboard converted into a house of worship. Lucy is suddenly quiet. She looks at the front doors, and then takes out her compact and reapplies a coat of pink lipstick.

The small gravel lot only holds about a dozen cars and with our arrival it is maxed out. I glance at the lighted entrance. Through the drizzled windshield I can just make out UNITED CHURCH. Two small, birdish women huddled under a single umbrella make their way in.

"Okay. I'm ready." Lucy tugs the door handle.

I pull up the hood of my coat, jump out, and run back to the trunk. Hauling out her walker, I wheel it to the passenger side before I pop her umbrella. Lucy takes hold of the walker and hoists herself up. She pauses again and pats her hair. "Do I look okay?"

"Beautiful."

She smiles as if it's not raining, sets her purse on the seat of the walker, and shoves off toward the front doors. It's not coming down all that heavy now but I walk alongside holding the umbrella centered over her head.

As we get closer, I notice that the stained-glass window is not the usual depiction of saints, but flowers and doves and a kind of cross I've never seen—it has two curved hooks at its base, like an anchor. Above the door, the sign says UNITED CHURCH OF SPIRITUALISM.

Spiritualism. The word knocks around my head—that old canard people like to trot out: *I'm not religious, but I am a spiritual person.*

Light and heat wash over us as I open the door.

"I'm here, Lloyd," Lucy says and pushes her walker inside.

That's when it begins to sink in. Spiritualism—talking to the dead. Messages from the dearly departed.

I fold the umbrella, dump it into the stand. Just inside, a wooden box is set on a small table. The lid has a three-inch slit and a sign reads: $5 SUGGESTED DONATION. Lucy stuffs in a folded ten-dollar bill and I follow her as she rolls through the vestibule toward the chapel.

About fifteen people are scattered around twelve pews in the small room, some staring straight ahead, hands clasped in their laps, while others hang over the backs of their seats and chat with neighbors. I have, of course, heard of spiritualism, but I didn't imagine it happening in a church. If I'd had to put a picture to a gathering like this, it would have involved a round table, dim lights, and a Ouija board.

"I can understand why you don't go to church anymore," Lucy tells me again, "but this is different." I'm hoping she'll pick a back pew, but she keeps on going up the center aisle and stops at the third row. "It's not like the Catholics. They ordain women here."

Once she's seated, I fold her walker and start for the back of the room.

"No. Keep that here. I like it close by."

"Won't it get in the—"

"Just fold it and rest it beside us."

I do as I'm told, lean the walker against the pew's end, and sit down next to her.

"Catholics," she says, and shakes her head. "Even the Episcopalians say that creed of theirs, 'I believe in one holy blablabla Catholic Church!' They start their services with it!"

Looking up at the wooden rafters, I pick at a hangnail and say, "That's *catholic* with a small *c*. *Catholic* just means 'inclusive'—it means 'universal.'"

"I was kidding," Lucy says. "You're so sensitive." She looks around as if she is changing the subject. She leans over to me and whispers, "Some of them can be a little nutty in this place, so I like to sit by myself."

On the right is an organ. The pulpit is on the left. Don't know why I find this churchy setup so surprising.

"I used to take the Seniors TransRide out here, but it always brought me so damn early and I'd get stuck sitting around, talking to crackpots. I used to show them *Pennywhistle*." She opens the cotton bag in her lap enough that I can see the copy of her children's book. "People love it when I show them. 'Wow! I never met a real author before!' Makes them happy." She closes her bag and twists her head around to see who else might be here.

Sitting across the aisle in the first row is a woman wearing a hooded royal blue cape. She's resting against the pew end as she knits what looks to be a snood.

Lucy leans into me again. "That one in the blue cape, the one with the bad skin—*she's* Catholic. I met her at a channeling event. She used to give me a ride sometimes, but she's obsessed with medieval stuff. Knights in armor and all that crap. Thinks she's some reincarnated Lady of Camelot."

In the sanctuary are two soft armchairs, each bathed in a single shaft of light from fixtures directly above. The chair on the right holds a big woman, tall and thick, swathed in a violet pashmina. She had been ambling up and down the aisle a minute before, smiling and nodding. She gazes around the room now, sleepy-eyed.

Lucy gives me a light elbow in the side. "See that fat one sitting in the chair up front—she's the medium tonight. She's new, but she's good. Strange that someone can know so much about the afterlife and still be so fat."

I don't know what to say to that. I have no answer for much of what comes out of Lucy's mouth.

"Hello, everyone." A small, thin man walks to the space between the pulpit and the organ.

The woman in the blue cape puts her knitting down. Everyone settles in and faces the front.

"You'll like this guy," Lucy says. "He's cute."

"Welcome," the man says. "Thanks for coming out on such

a rainy night. For those of you who don't know me, my name is Danny. Why don't we start with a song? The first hymn tonight is number twenty-two in your books. 'Amazing Grace.' Shirley our organist couldn't make it tonight, but I think you all know the tune."

Beside me, Lucy opens a thin, spiral-bound hymnal and then she and the people around us begin to sing. I didn't expect them to sing about God in a place like this. "I once was lost but now am found," Lucy sings. She glances at me. I feel obliged to join in, but I can't. The sound of voices together like this always makes my throat go tight. Ever since I was a kid. It feels too big and sad somehow. So I stay quiet and move my lips.

When the song ends, Danny says, "Beautiful. You guys make my heart swell up!" He sets the mic down on top of the organ. "I'd rather skip the microphone when there is such an intimate little group. Can everyone hear me all right?"

"We can hear you!" Lucy shouts. A couple of heads in the first two rows turn to look at her. Some smile, murmur agreement.

Danny grins. "Great! We've got some good energy in the room tonight. I can feel it!" He tells us that he is from the Cree Nation and that he grew up in a family who was very much involved in the spirit. As a shaman himself, he has done a lot of work with healing circles, especially using the healing vibrations from gongs.

I can feel my brother roll his eyes. Ever since we were kids, Francis has believed in *one God, the Father Almighty* and *one holy Catholic and Apostolic Church.* He is definitely a capital-*C* Catholic. He told me a joke once that went: A Catholic gets stranded on a deserted island. After a few years, someone else comes to the island and notices that the castaway has built two chapels. The castaway explains, "This is the church I go to, and that is the church I'll never go to."

"I was named True Coyote Walker by the elder who taught me," Danny says. "The main message from my teacher has always been a question: Where are you going? What are you going to do?" He looks around the room. "The question from my teacher is a question from the Great Spirit: How do we let go of fear and pain and move forward? Right?"

"Right!" shouts Lucy. She gives me another nudge.

I move my butt a couple of inches away from her, I hope out of elbow range.

"There was once a man in one of my healing circles," says Danny. "The man was very depressed." He pauses to let those words sink in. "When someone is that depressed, the next step up isn't *happy*. It's too hard to believe in happy when you are down in that dark, dark place. I asked him the Question: 'Where are you going?' He was so depressed he didn't have an answer. So I reframed the Question. 'Where is better than here?' Sometimes we forget that moving forward comes in little steps. For someone down so low, that one little step might be anger. Anger isn't happy but it's sure closer to happy than depressed is."

I shift around. As an angry person, sitting in this pew, I find it very difficult to contain the agitation I feel hearing True Coyote Walker and his question from the Great Spirit. I'm so sick of religious quacks. No one wants to admit the most likely scenario: This is all you get. You get what you get and no amount of rage or providence is going to change it. I don't know what's worse: some Very Reverend Father Know-It-All telling me to pray harder or Sweat Lodge Danny here inviting me to listen to the Great Spirit.

Beside me, Lucy is riveted. Maybe I'm just jealous. I want to believe in something. Anything. Of course, tonight isn't about me and my pissy little opinions. Lucy is paying me twenty bucks an hour to be present and pleasant, to help her get from point A to point B and back again. That's it. That's my job.

She glances at me, smiles, her expression almost beatific.

Smile back. Breathing through my nose I remember to force the corners of my mouth up, feel my cheeks crowd my eyes a little.

Mr. Coyote Walker is talking about meditation now. He says he is going to lead the room in a guided meditation using the vibrations of the gong.

He pulls two stands with him into the center of the sanctuary. There are four gongs, two sets of two, one suspended above the other. He picks up a mallet with a soft, bulbous head. Around me, people close their eyes. I glance at Lucy, who is already breathing deeply, eyes closed.

Just do your job. Present and pleasant.

I close mine too.

A soft, low thrum, and the room fills with tremulous vibrations that I feel so bone-deep, my eyes snap open. No one else seems bothered.

Shut them again. Faking it works.

Another gentle punt of a gong and the air ripples against my skin like lake water. Just breathe. Who's it going to hurt?

I take in the reverberating air and let it tremble through my lungs. A lower vibration from another gong joins the first.

Thoughts drift to Francis, long ago trying to tell me the reason for ritual, the smells and bells, the solemn visceral chants that transport the mind to somewhere it doesn't normally go. It begins to feel as if my frame is melting against the pew.

Long, slim strains weave through the reverberations, fading into a gentle tide so warm and thick, it's as if I am floating in a womb filled with honey.

Then it comes, the soft hint of his breath in my ear. Milky, warm breath. The sense of him reverberates like another gong. I'm awake but it isn't scary this time. He can be here. He belongs here. The weight of him, the feel of Frankie's little bum settling into my lap, his warm back against my chest—I want to hold him, to touch his warm fingers, but the only way to keep him here is to keep still. I know it.

Soon the gongs ease, but the vibrations linger. Frankie's head thumps gently against my clavicle, the wisp of his fine hair under my jaw. I can't look. I won't.

There is a long silence. A genuine smile creeps onto my lips and if I cry tonight it will be something different, something like bliss and love and sky and fullness. I wish I could dissolve into this sensation and never come back.

A woman's voice slips quietly into my mind and at first I wonder if I have created her. "My name is Reverend Kalinda Fetherling. I am a medium," she says. "This is the portion of our evening where we connect with spirit. I will ask you if you want a message. Say yes, no, or maybe. Please don't nod

if you don't understand. Okay? I have someone here. This
spirit who is with me . . . I'm getting a name like Joan, or Jen.
Maybe Jan—she wants to speak to the lady with the earrings.
You, yes. Does this J-name make sense to you?"

A couple of rows back, a voice says, "Yes! It's Jan!"

"Jan. Yes, Jan is here with us tonight. She has such a rush of
love for you. She says, 'I'm really doing all right. You should
see the place!' I get the sense that she wasn't able to do a lot
with her space when she was here—Does this make sense to
you? Yes? But she has everything now. She knows now that
those things weren't important, but you were important. 'I
should have faced up to it,' she says, 'loved you and hugged
you and thanked you. And wow, things are going okay with
you too. Wonderful things!'"

"Yes, I can feel her."

I am drifting with Frankie. Sleepwalking between worlds,
curled around the heat of him. Listening and drifting.

"Is your grandmother in spirit?" the medium asks.

Behind me, a voice answers, "Yes."

"I think that's who I have with me. 'I'm not alone,' she says.
'I'm being well looked after. I just wanted to come back and
tell you that I'll always be there for you.' She says she worked
really hard to make herself heard by you. She says, 'Would
you tell your mother about my visit today? Because I come
to her and your mom feels sad and I want her to feel love.'"

Somewhere near there are quiet sniffs.

"Another presence is with me," the medium says. "May
I come to you? Yes, in the red sweater. I'm feeling energy
around the heart. This person had some issue with heart or
respiratory. It's a breathing thing, asthma or bronchitis. Does

this make sense to you? Yes? This is a lady coming through. She's short, five foot three or so. Slender. Does this make sense to you? No? Maybe? Oops, she's laughing! Really? She's telling me she was a little rounder in life. Does this make sense to you? She says she carried so many things, issues, and worries and that you're a little mirror of her, that you take on too many worries. 'Let it go,' she says, 'don't wait like I did.' You need balance. Is your mother in spirit? Yes? This is your mother I have with me."

The voices are getting quiet and quieter. Soon I can't hear anything but a soft pulse in my ears. In our ears. We are dreaming together, we are dozing, drifting, Frankie and me. He needs me. What would it take to be here with Frankie forever?

A thump in my ribs—my body is quaking. I gasp back into the room. Lucy has me by the thigh, jostling me.

"She has a message for you!" Lucy says.

He's gone. No. Please no. My Frankie is gone. Chased off by this crazy old bitch. I want to slap her. I want to snap her in half.

"Can I come to you?" Kalinda stares at me, her purple pashmina draping off extended arms.

"I—yes." A rush of heat comes up my arms and legs. I can't do this. "I mean, no. No, I can't." My heart is slamming. I'm on my feet, sidestepping out of the pew.

"Please don't be frightened," Kalinda says. "Some people—"

"Excuse me. I need some air."

"It's okay," Lucy says. "You're just—"

Before she can finish I am heading down the aisle, out of the church and into the rain.

FIVE

Ben

The old man screamed. Blood spattered on the sheets. Ben and Cola stood in the hospital corridor just outside his room. Two male nurses, one on either side of his bed, tried to feed a tube up his nose and down his throat. He'd yanked it and now they had to get it back in. Had to keep his stomach drained.

"Relax, Mr. Brody. You're just making it harder on yourself."

"Fuck you, you little prick."

Hard to make out with no teeth in his head, but Ben heard him loud and clear.

The old man had pulled the IV from his arm twice. If he got his hands on the one in his neck, the walls would be washed in red. His wrists and ankles were in restraints now. A chest vest kept him trussed to the bed.

The nurses went for round two. "Come on, Mr. Brody, swallow, swallow!"

"No. No!" The old man let go a shriek as if there were hooks tearing out his entrails. Maybe he thought there were.

"Jesus Christ!" Cola said. He made a move and Ben grabbed his arm, held him steady. Cola pushed him off. "Come on, man, why do they have to hurt him like that? It's fucked-up."

"It's for his own good," Ben said, because you can't say, Karma's a bitch. He nodded down the hall. "Come on. I'll buy you a drink."

THE TWO OF them sit on a green vinyl couch in front of the coffee machine. Each holds a paper cup; neither says a word. There's a hand sanitizer on the opposite wall. A sign says, CLEAN YOUR HANDS. IT'S YOUR DUTY. On the other side of the dispenser is an Alzheimer's poster: "Caring for a loved one with dementia impacts every aspect of your life."

Five days after surgery and the old man still can't understand what he's doing here. Can't retain it. The nurses have asked if he's got a history of dementia. Between the tranquilizers and the cough syrup, who knows?

"How come you never told me he was throwing up?"

"I told you. I did! Not right away because he said not to." Cola's eyes are watery. They slide up and down the hall. "I didn't want to hurt your feelings, man. He said, 'Don't tell Ben cuz he'll just come stompin' in here and tell me what to do.'"

Another anguished howl echoes down the hall. Cola's hands are shaking, his pupils so big and black there's no iris. Ben would take it for sympathy if it weren't for those eyes. Cola's eyes look the way they did the time the old man kicked down the door. They look like they did when their mother finally walked out for good.

Miriam would only be about sixty-five now. Ben figures she must be dead. How else could she disappear so completely? Cola claims he saw her on the street once, standing on the corner across from the school yard. She was watching him, he said. A big moving truck came round the corner and blocked his view. He jumped down from the monkey bars and ran to the fence. By the time the truck cleared, she was gone.

Cola still scans the faces of women in the street. When he meets a new girl, he asks her how old her mother is, what her mother's first name is. He asks if her mother can sing. That's the only thing he seems to remember: Miriam had a very pretty singing voice.

When the old man was out, Miriam liked to put the radio on in the kitchen and sing along. She liked the oldies—the Beatles and Bobbie Gentry. There's one afternoon Cola still keeps in his pocket: Gold light dropped in through the window over the kitchen sink. It packed along its very own song and Miriam knew all the words. *We'll sing in the sunshine,* she crooned, a smile in her voice. Cola giggled each time she got to the bit about laughing every day. He reached for her hands and she waltzed him in circles.

We'll sing in the sunshine. That's Cola's Miriam.

Of course, Ben had her for longer. Before Cola came on the scene Ben would go to work with her. Two or three years old, trailing behind, hand on the tail of her coat as she dragged the yellow janitor's pail around the deserted football stadium. He would stand against the wall, eye level with the sinks, and watch her scrub toilet after toilet, urinal after urinal, before she started mopping the floors.

After Cola was born, there was no money for a sitter, so Ben stayed home to look after him while Miriam and the old man went to work. The old man cleaned the floors in public schools. Before that he had a factory job, making tar and concrete—until he crushed his thumb filling drums with hot tar from the spigot. He took what he could get: resentful kinds of work, the kind where you didn't need an education.

Ben would also be in charge at night when his parents went to Shelly's pub across the road. No matter how broke, there was always money for drinking.

"Okay, little man," his mother would say. "We'll sit where we can see your bedroom window. If it's an emergency, turn the light on. No screwing around."

Ben was five. He liked giving Cola his bottle, liked the way his round brown eyes stared up. Like worship. Like he would love him forever.

The diapers were tough, though—getting those sticky tapes right. One time Ben fucked up the last Pampers in the house. Miriam was at work. The old man was home that day, in front of the TV with a beer, and he didn't want to hear about it.

In the bedroom, Ben looped his father's belt around the diaper but it wouldn't stay. Cola crapped himself again. It was getting on the bed. Holding the diaper together, Ben hauled the baby to the bathroom. He put him in the tub. The diaper fell off. Cold tub against his butt, Cola started to cry. The old man made Ben close the bathroom door so he wouldn't have to listen to the racket.

When Miriam came home, she found Cola in the tub covered in shit and wailing blue murder. "You leave a baby like this?" She swatted Ben's head. She snatched the TV remote out of the old man's hand. "You couldn't put a clean diaper on him?"

"I don't clean other people's shit. That's your line."

She aimed the remote and turned off the tube.

"Who the hell do you think you are?" His dad looked at her as if she were something stuck to his shoe.

"I'm the one you'll never see again if I walk out that door."

Miriam wasn't going anywhere, the old man said, because no one would have a bitch like her who stank of shit.

It was the same roaring match. The old man would send Ben outside—"Go play!" When Cola was big enough, they both left.

Miriam never had a black eye. Not that Ben could remember. There was a split lip once. She said she'd opened the kitchen cupboard and a can fell out.

The night of Ben's tenth birthday, she made good on her threat to walk out. Miriam dragged the two boys and a suitcase about ten blocks east to the cheapest flophouse she knew. Cola tripped over every curb and cried the whole way. "Just say you're sorry and he won't be mad anymore," he pleaded.

The place was called the Parisienne. The lobby smelled like mold and beer. The geezer behind the desk made lizard eyes at Miriam as she rooted in her purse for the first night's rent. Ben stared at the lump in the pouch of his cheek. The man's mouth opened, and his tongue moved the lump down front. He pulled a crusty red hankie from his sleeve and wiped spittle from the corners of his lips.

Miriam handed him a ten and five ones. "Do you need any help around here?" she asked. "Cleaning? I do a good job."

He picked up the black plastic ashtray beside the cash register and spat a wad of wet chaw into it. "So do I."

That night, Miriam, Ben, and Cola lay in the dark on a double bed. "When are we going home?" Cola asked. No answer. He asked Miriam if she'd sing a song. There was a long pause. Then her voice came low and sweet. "We'll sing in the sunshine," she sang. When she came to the second verse, the bit about kissing you morning and night, someone hammered the wall. "Shut up!"

None of them spoke again.

Hours later, Ben lay awake, listening to traffic and staring at slits of street light on the walls. When footsteps echoed in the hall, he watched the chain on the door, tensing, waiting.

The next morning, Miriam went down to the lobby. She came back with a small carton of chocolate milk, poured it into two glasses from the bathroom, and handed one to each boy. "He says he's sorry," she said.

"I told you," Cola said.

They weren't home a week before the fights started up again. Soon Miriam and the boys were back at the Parisienne.

Two nights into their second stay, the desk clerk knocked at the door. She had a phone call, he said.

Miriam opened the door. "I'm not here."

The old clerk looked from her to the boys. He moved the chaw from one side of his mouth to the other. "You owe for tonight," he told her and scuffed back down the hall.

As soon as she closed the door, Cola started in. "Why can't you just say you're sorry?"

She stared at him. Her mouth opened. Her face looked

like a memory—Ben recalled someone kicking over her yellow janitor pail, telling her to clean it up. He wondered who that was.

Cola's face turned red, tears rolling. "I hate it here. It stinks like barf. And there's mean, drunk people."

"There's mean, drunk people at home," Miriam said.

The three of them lay in the double bed that night. Cola slept. Miriam fidgeted. She rolled onto her side and faced Ben. They looked at one another until she finally spoke. "Do you think I should go back to him?"

She looked as if she truly believed he'd have the answer.

"I don't know," he said.

She stared into his eyes. "What if nobody else wants me?"

THE NEXT EVENING Miriam, Ben, and Cola had dinner in the room. No hot plate in there. They sat on the bed with a block of Velveeta and a loaf of Wonder. Miriam cut an apple into slices with a paring knife. "Sing the song about sunshine again," Cola said. Miriam smiled. Footsteps echoed in the hall. The familiar drag of the foot: heavy and angry. She shot a look at Ben.

The door thundered. All three of them stiffened.

"Miriam, open up." The old man banged his fist on the door again.

Off the bed, Miriam clutched the paring knife, her tongue flicking at her bottom lip as if she were working out a problem.

"Daddy?" Cola called. He ran to the door as the old man shouted, "Miriam, you open this goddamn door!"

Miriam yanked Cola back by his sweatshirt.

The old man's boot hit the wood and the door shook in

its frame. In the short quiet that followed, Ben thought he heard the sound of safety chains grazing locks on nearby doors. He wondered where the clerk was, if the police would come. He climbed off the bed and stood near the window.

"Miriam, I know you're in there."

"Daddy!" Cola struggled to get away from his mother.

A boot hit the door again. Just as Miriam turned away, it flew open, caught her in the shoulder, and knocked her and Cola to the floor. The knife dropped out of her hand and slid.

The old man stumbled in, panting. He picked up Cola. "Hey, boy." He held him and ordered Miriam over his son's shoulder. "Get your things." He set him down and scooted him toward the suitcase.

Cola looked at his mother. "It's okay, Mommy." He tried to help her up.

The old man had her by the hair before she made it to her feet. "You get your things."

"Don't touch me!" Miriam shrieked.

Ben stayed back against the windowsill, unsure whether to charge like a bull or duck out the door and disappear for good.

"Daddy, no, it's okay." Cola grabbed his father's free hand, stroked it, and patted it.

Miriam dove against the old man's side and bit hard until he threw her across the floor.

He snatched the knife off the floor.

Cola hung off his arm. "Daddy! Please. We miss you. We're sorry."

"See that," the old man said. "My *boys* love me."

Miriam got back on her feet and bolted through the open door. Her screams echoed. Nobody answered.

Ben moved toward his father. "Dad, we're coming. Just leave her alone. Give me the knife, okay."

The old man went out into the hall. "Miriam. You get back here. Get these boys' stuff together and get your ass home."

No sign of Miriam.

"You'll be sorry if I hafta find you."

At the end of the hall, two sets of slow footsteps came up the stairs, the sound of stiff, squeaking leather.

The old man threw the knife into the room. His voice turned pussycat when he said, "Evening, Officers. Sorry about the commotion. My boys—"

"Are you a resident here, sir?"

"It's a funny situation, I—"

"Would we find your name on the register? No? Sir, I think we should take this outside."

Ben watched out the window as the two cops talked to his old man on the sidewalk. Cola had followed after his father and stood next to him, staring up, flop of hair falling in his eyes. Soon the cops were talking more to Cola than his father. Minutes later, he was in the driver's seat of the squad car with an officer's cap on his head.

Heads turned as Miriam came out from hiding. Stepping onto the sidewalk she tucked in close to the nearest cop. The old man said something to her and held out his hands as though he were trying to reason. She went to the driver's side of the car, got Cola out, and pulled him in against her side.

Cola wriggled free. He ran to hug his dad goodbye and the old man walked off toward home.

THE THREE OF them stayed in the same room that night with a dresser pushed in front of the broken door. The next morning, Miriam packed their bags.

"Are we going to see Dad?" Cola asked.

No answer. They went out the back door of the hotel and walked the ten blocks home.

Miriam steered them into the apartment building and sat them down on the beat-up leather couch in the lobby.

Ben stared at the elevator. "They spelled it wrong," he said.

"ShitT HoLE" was sprayed in scrawling letters across both elevator doors, strings of orange paint drooling to the floor.

"He'll be home soon." She looked at the front door. She looked at the ceiling as if he might be there now. "He'll be glad to see you."

"He'll be glad to see everybody." Cola swung his legs out and thumped them back against the couch. The springs creaked.

Ben stared up at his mother. She looked away. He watched her throat move as she swallowed. Her thin blond hair was short and spiky up front, the back pinned up in a little bun. She was ten years younger than the old man but she had the same bags under her eyes, the same deep creases around her nose and mouth. As if he'd infected her.

Miriam went into her purse and handed Ben a five-dollar bill. "Get a hamburger for you and your brother."

"Are you going out again?" Cola asked.

She opened her mouth as if she were going to say goodbye, and then turned and walked out.

Ben watched the door close behind her. He listened to the steady thump-thump of Cola's heels against the couch. "We'll sing in the sunshine," he sang, and the two of them listened to it echo up the walls.

FIVE

Maggie

Huddled beneath the overhang of the United Church of Spiritualism, I stare into the rain as it drops through the streetlight. I check and recheck my watch. Figuring the service is just about over, I head back inside and wait at the back of the room.

There are a lot of damp eyes and smiles among them. As the offering plate circulates, they start singing "I'd Like to Teach the World to Sing." It's the real thing, they sing. What the world wants today.

A Coca fucking Cola commercial! That's their idea of a hymn?

After a few closing words from the medium, the congregation stands, joins hands, and rocks from side to side as they warble "Let There Be Peace on Earth."

"It can be overwhelming," Lucy says on the drive home. "The first time you get a message. My first time, when Lloyd spoke to me, I bawled my eyes out. A medium named Mo-nique Fontaine. She's the best."

I stare ahead at the road.

"This one tonight wasn't bad, though. After you left, she said she could feel your sensitivity and, you know, very often, sensitive people have the gift of second sight! I'm very sensitive and I could spot it in you right away. That's why I thought you and I might make a good team. I just had a feeling. I trust my feelings because they're usually dead-on."

Oh, please! Was there anyone in the room whose "sensitivity" that medium *didn't* feel? Anyone who *didn't* have a dead grandmother? Fuck them.

I don't say a word of that. I don't say a word.

It's nine thirty as we turn the corner onto Lucy's block.

"Why don't you go ahead and take the car," she says. "It's miserable out. I don't want you waiting for a bus in this rain."

"No. I can't take your car."

"Take it! You can bring it back in a couple of days."

I don't want it. I don't want Lucy. Or her jerk-off, psychic friends. But the rain is coming down in torrents. She pays me eighty dollars for the night and I do as I'm told.

I'M IN HER old gray Volvo now, out in front of my apartment, clenching and unclenching my jaw as I stare through the rain-splattered windshield. Is this where Ben parked? Was he in our car or was he driving one of the limos? In my mind, Ben is sitting in our crummy old beater, looking at the mailboxes, just the way I am now. I picture him scrawling a cryptic note to me on the back of a torn envelope, and then stuffing in two hundred dollars. He gets out of the car, goes over there, and crams the envelope into my mailbox. Was he thinking about doing it then? Did he have the gun already?

When I imagine it, the steel of the barrel, the cool of it against his skull, finger on the trigger, I get a suck of terror in my chest and I don't know whether it will come out as rage or more tears.

Fuck you, Ben. Fuck you fuck you fuck you for being such a goddamn self-hating jackass! My head drops against the steering wheel and I let the tears stream until the fire in my brain turns to a pile of steaming ash again.

At least he's alive. He's not in a coma or paralyzed. The bullet lodged in his skull. If it had been a greater caliber, they said, it would have been different. After they removed the bullet, I saw him in the recovery room, sleeping off the anesthetic. When I called the next day, they said he'd been moved to the psych ward. Standard procedure with attempted suicide.

I couldn't go back. I couldn't face him. It's been nine days now.

I don't know what to do with the claws in my belly anymore.

I want to be good. I want to love the memory in my lap and be grateful that I had Frankie for the two and a half years I did.

Pulling tissues from my purse, I wipe my face and blow my nose.

At last the rain stops. Out of the Volvo, I lock the doors and look up at my lighted apartment. Francis crosses the window. Father Luke: man of the cloth, brother of the bottle.

Mail key out, I check the box on the way up the walkway. Nothing but junk. A car door clunks open somewhere behind me. Slams shut.

"Excuse me!" A woman's voice. "Maggie MacDonald?"

I turn and see her trotting across the road toward me.

My stomach twists. Christ, what now?

"Katie Wilks from the *Herald*. I'm hoping to talk to you about your brother, Luke. Father Luke MacDonald is your brother, isn't he?"

I look at her extended hand and then up at my apartment. Francis passes by the window again. "I'm not ah—No. I have nothing to say."

"Please, just give me a second. I know how you must feel after what the police did to him." She puts her palms together as if she's praying to me. "Let me tell your side of the story. I know a lot about your family and—"

"You don't know me." I start off toward the front door and then stop. "What made you think he'd be here?"

"Father Michael, the rector at Holy Trinity. He said that it made him sick how the media was treating Father Luke."

My mouth hangs open and Katie Wilks makes a rapid-fire attempt to fill in the blanks. "He said that Father Luke is a good man, and that his parents died in a car accident when he was eighteen years old. Father Luke was left to care for his sister, Maggie. You're Maggie. You're—" She pauses for a moment. "You're the woman whose child fell from the window."

My hand flies out and shoves her back two steps. "Father Michael? That sonuvabitch told you that? He told you about my—? What kind of—"

"No! I was assigned to that story. When I heard Father

Luke's name something tweaked and it dawned on me. I checked the funeral notices for the church and sure enough, your brother—Father Luke—presided at the funeral."

I turn from her and storm up the walk to the front door.

Her footsteps follow me. "Maggie, please. I want to help."

"Sure you do." My key is in the lock.

"I think the police department should be held accountable. Public opinion is on your side. Listen, just take my card."

"Go to hell." I pull the door closed behind me and dash upstairs.

As I open the door to my apartment, I can hear sitcom music, the opening strains of *The Golden Girls'* theme song.

Francis is sitting on the couch opening a bottle of red wine.

"Are you kidding me?" I stare from the bottle to the geriatric women on the screen and back. "Are you fucking kidding me?"

"What's up your ass, Mother Manguard?" He picks his burning cigarette up off the ashtray.

I shake my head—"Idiot!"—and storm into my closet-of-a-bedroom.

Seconds later, there's a tap. Francis opens my door. "What is going on?"

I open my mouth and shift my jaw sideways, trying to release some tension, keep from exploding. "You want to know what's up my ass? You! Some reporter just jumped me out front. Why? You! She found you and she found me all in one fell swoop. Thanks to the rectum at Holy Trinity. Father Luke and his sister, Maggie, whose child—She knew. And then I pushed her. She's probably going to charge me with assault."

"Shit. I'm sorry, honey. I'm really sorry." He looks down at the smoke curling off his cigarette and then takes a drag. He sighs and stares at me a moment. "How did it go tonight?"

"How do you think it went? That old woman is a narcissistic little windbag—and then I come home to the asshole out front and now the asshole on my couch!" I gesture past him to the wine on the coffee table. "Are you really this stupid? Really?"

His eyes roll. "Don't be so dramatic. It's not like I'm driving."

"Sweet Jesus." I hug my ribs and roll back on the bed. "You're such an asswipe!"

Francis leans against the door frame. "Listen, sister, it took all my nerve to leave this apartment. I wore a pair of your old glasses and a hat and I went out the back door, got in my car, and headed to the nearest, smallest, darkest liquor store I could find. It's a shitty, rainy night, but I thought, after your first day back at work, you'd like a glass of wine. I thought I was doing something nice."

"Yeah, I'm sure you did." I rub my hands over my forehead and eyes. Eventually I look at him. "I'm scared for you, Francis."

"Me too," he says. He gives me a soft, lost smile and nods behind him.

Eventually, I get up, follow Francis to the couch, and flop down beside him. "I'm not drinking with you."

"Mags, honey, in a few days I'll be in rehab or jail so let's just be here now." He mashes the butt of his cigarette in the ashtray. Picking up the bottle, he tilts it toward the two empty wineglasses.

He sticks a full glass in my hand. Then he plucks up his

own, looks deeply into the burgundy pool, and says, "Hello, old friend."

I stare at my glass for what feels like minutes. Christ. Why bother? Can't stop him. Can't change him. Taking a sip, I glance up at Bea Arthur holding court on television.

Years ago, when Francis was still in the seminary he bought tickets to Bea Arthur's one-woman show. He invited me but I declined. I told Francis that he was a queer cliché. A few days after the show, he came over to my place for coffee.

"Now, my darling Margaret, you're going to see what you missed." He looked so damn proud of himself as he passed snapshots one at a time over my kitchen table. Turned out he had talked his way backstage and each image held the proof: Francis in Ms. Arthur's dressing room, arm across her shoulders, his big white teeth the perfect accent to her big white hair.

"Yikes. She's starting to look like Phyllis Diller," I said. "How'd you get in there?"

"St. John Chrysostom wasn't the only one with a golden mouth, darling." My brother winked.

I looked at him. "What?"

"Chrysostom . . . *golden mouth*? Ah, skip it."

He looks at the TV now and sighs at Bea Arthur. "It's sad that she's gone." He takes a sip of his wine, looks over, and picks a bit of lint from my sweater. "What happened tonight? Where'd you go?"

"The United Church of Spiritualism."

His eyes splash wide. "Nice!" He leans close and whispers, "Did you see dead people?"

"I saw dumb people—all of them listening to some woman give messages from the beyond." I glaze my eyes theatrically as if entering a trance. "*I have someone with me. It's a woman. You— the gentleman with the cigarette—can I come to you? She says you're a smoker—does this sound like you? A verbal answer, please: yes, no, or kiss my ass. Did you have a great-grandmother? Did her name start with A? B? How about C or F or M—M? Yes, was her name Martha or Madeline? Mary? No shit, that's who I've got here. Mary. Mary says she loves you and you work too hard. Does that sound like you?*"

Francis cackles. "So Lucy goes regularly?"

"Yes. And she's got the balls to sit there telling me how ridiculous the Catholic Church is."

Francis covers his mouth in mock horror. "That's awful. I can't imagine how you must have felt."

"Shut up. They stole my brother. I'm allowed."

Francis watches me for a few seconds. "Were you hoping? Just a little?"

I know what he's talking about. But I don't want to talk about what he's talking about.

Big gulp of wine—I grab the bottle and top up my glass, pause to stare at the label as though it's all very interesting before I set it back on the table.

My brother is still waiting.

"I feel him sometimes," I say at last. "Usually in bed, just as I'm waking up. He curls into my belly. Sometimes I'm wide awake and he climbs into my lap. I can feel him there, and I can smell his baby smell, his Frankie smell." I take another swallow. "I wonder if I'm losing my mind."

Francis lays his palm on my head. His hand smells of soap and nicotine. He tucks my hair behind my ear.

I duck away, and force a weak smile. "I don't want to get all weepy right now."

He takes his hand back and runs a finger along the rim of his glass. "Used to happen to me after Mom and Dad were killed," he says. "In the middle of the night, Dad would throw open my bedroom door and say, 'Where do you think you're going?' It was so real. And I'd bolt up and it'd be dark and still and so—empty. Then I'd remember. He never sounded angry. More jovial, you know. But I'd wake up terrified." My brother's big hands fidget with the stem of his glass. "I used to feel guilty that I never dreamed about her."

A long silence passes. I look at my brother's thick-lashed, sad eyes. "Did you mean it? That you were scared?"

"Who isn't?"

I turn away, and look at the television again, the odd sight of brawny Bea Arthur bent backward by a man who plants a big wet kiss on her. The canned audience hoots.

"Don't you ever miss . . . Don't you want to have a relationship? A life partner?" I keep my eyes on the screen. "You could go over to the Episcopalians. It's the same thing except they're okay with gay."

"You know what Bette Davis said?" Francis looks at the television too. "Gay liberation? I ain't against it, it's just that there's nothing in it for me."

I look at his profile a moment and wonder at the two of us, the choices we've made. It's too much to think about right now, so I sip my wine, let my head settle back, and close my eyes.

Ben

"For a guy who isn't Ben, you have a lot of access to Ben's memories," Dr. Lambert says. He waits.

What is that? What's that look on his face? Is that a mouthful of *Gotcha*?

"Growing up with a man like your father," he tries, "you must have made a lot of promises to yourself . . . what kind of man you would be, wouldn't be. When you think about fatherhood, what comes to mind?"

Comes to mind, out of mind, blow your mind. It's all bullshit, Freud shit, who gives a shit?

Lambert waits. For the other shoe to drop, for another word to pop. He folds his hands and sets them on his notes.

Go ahead. Two can play. First to blink, first to sink.

"Okay," he says finally. He looks at his watch. "Tomorrow there's a group session right about this time. If you'd rather, you can skip our session and go to group instead."

There's no Ben in group.

"You either are Ben or you're not," Lambert says. He's got his gotcha smile on again. "I think you know who you are. Why you don't want to be Ben? Give it some thought. We'll talk tomorrow."

WE'LL TALK TOMORROW. Today is *tomorrow* and it's Lambert time again. Already. From the door of the white, white room, you see it all—all the hall—and there's Lambert at the nurse's station, signing in, signing something. Sign of the times.

Ben o'clock. *You either are Ben or you're not.*

Fuck him. Rather join the circle jerk in the common room than listen to Lambert.

Lambert turns around. "Morning, Ben. You look like you might be heading over to Group." He smiles. Smug fuck. Never smile at a crocodile. "Well, good," he says. "Many hands make light work."

Many hands are the devil's tools. Give the devil a finger and he'll take the whole hand.

So, THIS IS Group. The group grope. The brain drain. Looking around the common room now, it is clear why many hands require a glass-enclosed nursing station and a locked ward. Home sweet home. A couple of guys were playing checkers in the corner earlier, but they picked up and left when the TV was turned off and ten group chairs were pushed into a circle.

Instead of Lambert, a guy who looks younger than Cola sits at the helm. He's got a clipboard in his lap. He flips through pages of notes as though a test is coming.

Including the guy with the clipboard, four of the ten

chairs are filled. A round brown woman in flannel panda bear pajamas and a long black China girl wig sits directly across. She pets the length of her hair and peers around the circle. Her eyes dart to the door as if it might suddenly close tight. One more locked door.

Two chairs from her is a man who shuffled in here in pajamas and socks. He hasn't shaved in a day or two, but he still looks clipped and slick. He looks like money.

"Today's group is a spirituality workshop," says the guy with the clipboard. "The emphasis will be human spirit. I promise there won't be too much God talk."

Why not? If anyone has something to answer for, it's the sonuvabitch upstairs.

Eyes glittering, Money watches the clipboard man. "Spirituality," he says. "Right. Good. Cuz that's exactly what I need—spirituality!"

The woman continues to stroke her wig as she leans sideways to get a better look out the window. She straightens up again. "You sure this is the group? Who are you?"

"My name is William," says the man behind the clipboard. "I'm a chaplain."

"I ain't dyin'," she says.

"I'm glad to hear that." William the chaplain clears his throat. "No, this is a group where we'll be talking about healing and hope."

Hope against hope. Abandon all hope.

William blinks. "Where there's life there's hope," he says.

That's what you call the old hope-a-dope.

William smiles and clears his throat again. "Why don't we go around and introduce ourselves? I'll start. As I said I'm

William. Delaney. I'm a seminarian, and a chaplain here at St. Anthony General."

Just what the world needs, another priest. Another preacher. Another smug bastard who claims he's got a direct line to the big man. Reverend, rabbi, imam: same shit.

"I'm Greg," says Money. "I'm an attorney. At least that's what I was before I realized what God wanted me to see—"

"I'm Keisha," the round one says.

There's a long pause. All eyes turn to the body still not spoken for.

"Would you like to introduce yourself?" William asks.

Nobody's business. Not open for business.

Who's that at the door? Was that Lambert peeking inside? Is that sonuvabitch spying? *You either are Ben or you're not.* Fuck him. Say it loud, say it proud: No self here. Just a skinbag. An empty windsock.

William waits a moment and then says, "I'm sorry to hear you say that. You must be hurting a lot to feel that way." He gathers himself and carries on with the spiel. "In this group we can talk about anything you want to talk about, but usually I ask people if they could share something about their personal stories—and maybe your feelings about hope and healing." William looks around the circle. "What gives you hope? Or what might be preventing you from feeling hope?"

"Yes!" says glittering Greg. "I definitely feel hope."

Keisha gives Greg the once-over and then turns back to William. "We going t'talk about God?"

"God is real," says Greg. "I found that out this week. God is real and the soul is real. Evil is real too. There's evil stalking the earth. The Antichrist. And nobody sees it."

He says this all in one breath, as if he is unloading a magazine on the room.

Keisha looks back at the door. "Uh-huh. There's dark forces out there. The devil has black arts he uses and it really messes with people."

Greg looks at her. "You're right. People don't realize what's going on—and I'm going to help change that. God wanted me to see. So I could prepare myself."

Keisha stares past William to the window. She leans to the side again as if there's something she's trying to keep an eye on. She bolts upright, stands and points to a building across the street. "He's going to jump!" she shouts.

All eyes turn. Nothing out there but sealed office windows.

Keisha sits down. She picks up another swatch of long black wig hair and stares closely at the ends.

Greg winces. He rubs his palms on his pants. His lips pull back like a mad dog when he says, "The mayors, governors, senators—they're all—they don't know what needs to be done. They have to go. Then I'll be next in line." He pauses as if he's laying it out as simply as possible. "The man in charge needs to be slain. He's part man, part reptile. He's the Antichrist. I see that now. I know him."

William the chaplain's legs tense as if he's just heard breaking glass. He glances to the door and back at Greg. "It sounds like a lot is going on for you. A lot of turmoil?"

Greg nods. He doesn't take his eyes off William.

"That must be a lot to handle."

"It is," Greg says. "Nobody sees the evil—and it's right here."

Keisha nods.

William breathes through his nose. His eyes dart to the door once more. Who's he looking for? Lambert? You don't want Lambert in here, pal. You either are Ben or you're not. That's all Lambert's got.

"Keisha," William says, "you and Greg have talked about the power of darkness and evil. Do evil and suffering sometimes seem more real than goodness and healing?"

Greg sneers like he knows what's what. Preparing for the big reveal. Bastard must be a killer in the courtroom. "That," he tells William, "is a good question. God is powerful. But evil must be destroyed. That's what God revealed to me this week." Greg shrugs. "That I'm Jesus Christ."

Oh Christ, he thinks he's Christ.

Keisha rolls her eyes. "You ain't Jesus."

"Yes," Greg says with a flinty kind of elation. "I am. I was surprised too. But I am. They put nails into my hands and feet when they were bringing me in here. I fell forward and I smacked my head on the floor and they put nails in my hands and feet. That's when I began to realize I was Christ. I was right where I was supposed to be. My Father saw to it, and while I was being crucified, my mission became clear. I need to kill the Antichrist."

Christ, he says! Christ is the biggest bully of 'em all. You're Ben or you're not.

Keisha tucks her chin to her chest and says, "I need to get out of here. These people are caw-razy."

"That sounds scary, Greg," William says. "It also sounds like a lot of pain. Is that right?"

Greg closes his eyes and lowers his head. He begins to inhale slowly and deeply as if he's deliberating on each breath.

"What are you feeling right now?" William asks him.

Greg keeps his eyes shut. His breaths come deep and hard. "Anger," he whispers. He raises a pair of dog pit eyes to the chaplain. "Righteous anger. Like I could kill. It wouldn't be murder. It would just be killing evil." He takes another breath. "But I'm not going to kill. I just needed to let the Holy Spirit help me answer the question you asked. I don't think God wants anyone to suffer. Not even a man without a soul." He turns his head to Ben. "What did you call yourself? An empty skinbag? You think we can't see you. I see you. And I could find you anytime I wanted. The name outside your door says B. Brody. Benjamin Brody. I can find you anytime I want."

Benjamin isn't here. He's out in the desert wrestling with Christ until the sonuvabitch says uncle. You're Ben or you're not. See? Ben's been jumped by Jesus Christ. Jesus Christ was a warrior and you, Greg, are no Jesus Christ. If Ben were here right now, he'd tell Greg to take a flying leap out that window and see if the angels break his fall.

A woman comes into the room. She stands by the door and mutters something.

"What's she sayin'?" asks Keisha.

William turns to the door with his hope-eyes on. "Good afternoon! Are you coming in to join us?"

"Is this the spirituality group?" the woman says. In her early fifties maybe. Black jeans sag around her hips. Long gray sweater drips like water.

"Yes, it is," says William. "It's a group about hope and healing."

She looks like Bambi's mother with those skinny legs of hers. She comes to the circle and sits next to Keisha.

"Spirituality, that's right. I'm Greg." Greg, the Attorney, sticks out his hand like Christ looking for new clients. "What's your name?"

"Gwen." She starts to cry as soon as she says it. The fire in the room goes out with her tears. Cool and damp.

Greg jumps up and pulls tissues from the box on the table behind him. He hands them to her and sits down.

"Gwen," William, says. "Would you feel comfortable telling us what's brought you here."

"I just . . . I'm depressed. I can't—" She wipes her nose and shakes her head.

"Why are you depressed?" Greg asks.

Gwen looks into the knot of tissue. "Everything's gone. My husband tries to help me, but I just can't . . . My family, my place, my job . . ."

"You're in a lot of pain?" William asks. She nods. "Has this been going on for a while?"

"Since my son died."

Sons and sons and sons. For God so loathed the world that he snatched all their begotten sons.

"I'm so sorry," says William. "Can you tell us what happened?"

Greg closes his eyes and lowers his head, breathes slow and deep through his nose.

"I hadn't seen him in fifteen years," she says. "And then

I find out he's died. He killed himself. I didn't even know where he was."

Still grappling in the desert, Ben pauses, turns his head to listen. He squints to get a better look. Voices roil around him, they whip like a sandstorm, push into every orifice and deep into his lungs until Ben breathes the breath of every lost son of every lost mother in the world. The desert parts like a dry sea and he is once again staring into a gulf, standing at the edge with his hands against the moon. *Jump,* says Jesus. *Jump!*

SIX

Maggie

The wine bottle is long empty and Francis is curled up asleep, his head at the other end of the couch. I keep hearing his words. "I'd wake up terrified."

After our parents died, I clung to him. Francis was eighteen years old, just a kid. Then suddenly he wasn't. Just like that.

If I had to choose between instant death and a slow death, I would choose the latter. An instant shatters. An instant can tear down the world.

It was an eight-car pileup on a freeway just outside town. Our father had taken Mom to a bed-and-breakfast for her birthday. A weekend getaway at a country inn. According to police, the driver of the semitruck had been awake for twenty-two hours when he dozed off and crossed the yellow line. Our car was crushed. Paramedics said my parents' deaths would have been instant.

That's the word they used. As if a switch was flipped and the lights went out. No time to wish or pray or say goodbye. That word *instant* was meant to give us solace, I suppose. What it did was coil at the bottom of my belly like a rattlesnake: What could you prevent from happening in an instant? Could I get from one room to another in an instant? Could I have saved our world if I'd been in the backseat?

For the first couple of weeks after our parents died, I asked Francis if I could sleep in his bed. Even there, I had to keep a foot or a hand against him, as if that contact might be enough to give fair warning. I woke when he woke. I woke when he slept. I sat up in the dark and watched him. My brother's sleep was so quiet, so still, that sometimes I put a finger under his nose to check that he was breathing.

When I think of it now, Francis had a quiet fortitude through the entire aftermath. He put his head down and plowed through funeral arrangements, death certificates, and the notification of friends and family. In hindsight I wonder if my parents had a premonition: They made him the executor of their estate just after Francis turned eighteen. I imagine they figured he would be quite a bit older by the time he took on that role.

He arranged to sell the house; he paid off the mortgage, sold off furniture, and moved us into a two-bedroom apartment. He cooked dinner most nights. He said it was important that we be a family and that we continue to eat together the way we did when Mom and Dad were here. He wanted us in church too—which had not been the case when Mom and Dad were here. Our family was nominally Catholic. Francis and I had both been baptized, but in the past we'd only gone to Mass for Christmas and Easter, sometimes Palm Sunday.

Since the funeral, Francis wanted our butts in the pew every Sunday morning.

I didn't mind. I wanted plans. I wanted commitment. Commitment left less room for change. Which left less room for calamity. The more pieces that were locked into place, the fewer would fly off.

We'd been on our own for about two months when Francis asked, "How would you feel if I got a full-time job?" Between selling the house and paying off debts, Francis calculated that there would be enough cash to pay our rent for the next five years. But little else.

"Can't we just be careful?" I wanted him home; I wanted him where I could picture the walls around him.

Sometimes in the middle of a school day, my chest would feel as if there were something huge and terrible pressing on it, and I'd be certain that it was a sign. I'd have to excuse myself and race down the hall to the school's front entrance. My hands shook as I jammed quarters into the pay phone. They had to go in fast—in an instant. The surge of fear seemed to obliterate my thoughts so that sometimes seconds would pass where I couldn't recall my own phone number.

I learned to keep it written on my wrist. I wrote our number there every day the first year after they died. I needed to dial immediately. Had to.

Standing in the school lobby, I could hear my breath echoing off the twenty-foot ceiling. Francis must have heard the fear at the end of the line. "You okay?" he'd say in a calm, easy voice.

"I just wanted to make sure." That was all I needed. Just to hear his voice. Another instant thwarted.

"You could probably still call me at work," Francis said. "But I doubt I'll be able to walk you home from school anymore."

He did that sometimes. He'd walk down to the school and wait on the sidewalk out front.

"Whatever. I'm not five." Meanwhile my heart had begun to fling itself against the walls of my chest like a trapped squirrel.

Francis got a full-time job at Paulson's, a paint and wallpaper store five blocks from our apartment. It wasn't so bad. He still got me out of bed every morning and he was still home most nights for dinner.

And then we had Gale.

Francis called me from work one day and said that he was going to bring a friend home. Together, they would make dinner for us. "Gale makes the most incredible chicken you ever had in your life."

Gale. Shit. I drooped inside.

Francis had had a girl in high school, but they'd broken up just before he graduated. Three months later we'd lost our parents. And he'd been looking after me ever since. He was almost nineteen now. Having a girl in his life seemed like a potentially disastrous distraction, but I wanted him near.

If you accept his girlfriend, I reasoned, he won't want to go far.

Maybe she would be really cool and we could be friends. Maybe she'd have a cute brother and introduce us.

That night, Francis opened the door to our apartment with a bag full of groceries. "S'up, slob?" he said.

Sprawled in the armchair, I wore my usual TV-watching ensemble: saggy sweats and an old T-shirt.

"Hey, I'm Gale." Sunlight angled low through the window and Gale seemed to step into a warm spotlight.

He looked older than my brother. He wore jeans and a brown leather jacket over a crisp white shirt. His hair was thick and wavy and you could see his five o'clock shadow. He looked like TV to me, as if he spent hours trying to look casual.

"This is my pet loudmouth," Francis said and took the groceries into the kitchen.

"Pleasure to meet you." Gale came closer and shook my hand. "Francis, you never told me Maggie was such a cutie."

I folded my arms across my chest.

"That's no cutie, that's my sister." Francis came back into the living room.

My chest felt heavy, as if something were pressing again. What did Francis think he was doing, bringing a strange man into our apartment? A man named *Gale*. I muttered something about changing, got out of the chair, and went to my room.

We never had company. We didn't even know this guy. I looked in the mirror to see if I looked as awkward and scraggly as I felt. Gale was probably twenty-five years old. Maybe more. His voice echoed in my head. *You never told me Maggie was such a cutie.*

Was he flirting? He was too old to be flirting with me.

I leaned in close to the mirror and looked at my skin. My forehead was broken out. I pulled off my T-shirt and stared at myself: *Fifteen. I look fifteen.*

Hands on my boobs, I pushed them up: *I could probably pass for Francis's age. If I wanted to, I bet I could pass for nineteen.*

I went to my closet. What do you wear for company? Was I supposed to dress up? Maybe a white blouse and jeans. Like Gale.

I buttoned my top in the mirror. I put on lip gloss. And mascara.

Francis and Gale were well into dinner preparations by the time I came out. I leaned against the kitchen door frame and watched them. At the counter, Francis cut up tomatoes for a salad. Gale stood over the stove and turned his chicken pieces with a fork. Francis had given him my mother's apron to wear. It was kind of weird and goofy that Gale didn't mind wearing a woman's apron. Sweet, maybe. Maybe it was sweet and goofy.

"Nice outfit," I said. "You could probably moonlight as a French maid in that getup."

Gale stood back from the stove as grease splattered. "I see you speak fluent smartass. Must run in the family."

My brother gave me the once-over. "Don't you look darling."

I gave Francis a sarcastic bat of my eyes. I watched Gale's hands as they worked over the chicken. My brother's hands were kind of girly in comparison. "So how do you know a dork like Francis?"

My brother snorted. "Oh my God, she thinks I'm a dork. I think I'll cry."

"We work together," Gale said.

"Gale is the big cheese at the paint shop." Francis dumped his tomato slices into the bowl.

"You're his boss? You don't look old enough to own something."

Gale turned off the oven. "My pops and I own it together."
I nodded. "Do you get free paint?"

FRANCIS HAD ME lay an actual tablecloth. The way we used to do a million years ago. We put down place settings and napkins. We put out knives and forks and glasses. We even turned the television off.

Gale set two bottles on the table, one wine and one sparkling water.

"Fancy," I said. "How'd you get the wine?" The sight of it was almost as foreign as the water. "Oh, right. You're old."

"Maggie!" Francis said it just the way our mother would have.

Gale picked up one of those little bartender corkscrews, twisted it into the cork, and popped it like an expert. "Will the lady be sampling the Chardonnay this evening?"

It almost felt as though Gale were talking to someone his own age. I wished I had something clever to say. Not smart-ass, but really damn clever.

"The lady will be sampling the Perrier." My brother unscrewed the bottle of fizzy water.

"God, Francis." I rolled my eyes. "Don't be such a fag."

Gale glanced at me and heat flashed through my face. I hadn't meant anything by it. Francis and I said rude stuff to each other all the time. He called me all kinds of things: silly twat, goon-girl, fuck-knuckle. But tonight there was a stranger in the house and suddenly it sounded as if I had just thrown dog shit on the table.

My eyes welled up. I was ready to bolt. This was why we

should not have unexpected guests. This was why we should keep things in order.

Francis plunked his elbows on the table. "Listen, Liza." He meant Minnelli. Liza Minnelli was Francis-speak for being a drunken berserker. The inside joke was calming. "Listen, Liza," he said, "if I have to scrape your drunk ass off the floor one more time, we're through."

Gale laughed. I blinked at my brother and hoped he could read my remorse.

Francis poured Perrier into my wineglass.

"Thanks," I whispered.

GALE CAME OVER again on the weekend and brought movies with him. I sat on the couch between Francis and him with a bowl of popcorn in my lap as the coming attractions began.

"Have you guys seen these new DVD players?" Gale asked. "My uncle's got one. The whole movie is encoded onto a little silver disk this big." He circled his palm. "The picture quality blows this out of the water."

I looked at our VCR. My father had bought it about five years earlier. It was solid and real and it wasn't going any-where. "Why don't you go to your uncle's, then?"

"I like the company here better." Gale dug his hand in the popcorn bowl and my stomach flipped.

On my sixteenth birthday, Gale took the three of us for dinner. He bought a bottle of champagne for the table and Francis let me have a glass to myself.

"I'd like to make a toast." Gale raised his flute. "Cool, friendly, clever, beautiful . . ." He looked at me across the table. " . . . but enough about me. Here's a toast to Maggie."

He winked. His eyes were blue like denim. He looked as if he knew everything there was to know and still liked me. "Lovely Maggie," he said. "May you live a hundred years and may I live a hundred and one, so that I may remember you! Cheers, sweet girl."

"Look at her blush," Francis said. "Don't buy it. She's a wicked thing."

I giggled through the rest of the evening. At home, I drifted in my bed and directed little movies in my mind: Gale walking me home and taking my hand; Gale telling me that he knew there was a difference in our ages, but he had never met a girl like me; Gale kissing me; Gale touching me. "Gale and Maggie Paulson." Maybe Gale could introduce Francis to one of his cousins and Francis would fall in love and we could have a double wedding. We'd all live together in a big house and we'd paint the walls all kinds of crazy colors. Every night would be sure and simple and the same and we would never want it to change.

I ASKED MY friend Rhonda how old you had to be to have sex with a guy over twenty-one. We sat on the school grass at lunch hour. Rhonda had had sex twice. She'd done it with a guy our age and a twenty-two-year-old. "If you haven't lost it yet," she said, "then you definitely want to get yourself an older guy. These twinks don't know what the hell they're doing."

I told her about Gale. "He totally sounds optimum," she said.

"I don't want him to get in trouble. What's the age where no one could say a thing about it?"

"Seventeen," Rhonda said. "Once you're seventeen, you can do whatever you want with whoever you want and anyone who doesn't like it can get bent." She advised me to go on the pill.

Seventeen was only a few months away. Gale knew that. He was waiting. I could feel my face heat up as I thought about it. My stomach clenched. And then clenched again. Harder.

"Ouch. Fuck." It wasn't my stomach, more like my pelvis. I put my sandwich down.

"Cramps?"

"Yeah. My period started this morning, but—"

"You want a Tylenol?"

"Okay, yeah. Oh shit, oh no." I felt a sploosh as if a small dam had just burst.

"What!" Rhonda looked from my face to the clenched fist in my lap.

"I think I just sprang a leak." My face crumpled. We both looked down at my pale blue jeans.

"You want to stand up and I'll check?"

"Okay." I looked around to see that no one was paying attention. Another stabbing pain and I gasped and doubled over. "Holy shit. It feels like someone shoved a sword up my crotch."

Rhonda stared. "You didn't already fuck this guy, did you? I mean this couldn't be a miscar—"

"No! Stupid!" I kept my back to the tree and got up on my knees. "Just look, okay."

Rhonda leaned back to assess my backside. "Oh shit. You look like you just got shot in the ass."

"Fuck. Fuck fuck fuck. Oh! It hurts."

Rhonda took out a blister pack with four painkillers. "Here. Do you have more tampons?"

"I think I have to go home."

It was about one thirty in the afternoon when I came into our building. My sweatshirt was tied around my waist. I'd taken two of Rhonda's Tylenol but they hadn't done much. When I got to our door, it was clear that Francis was home. His Peter Gabriel album was on the stereo. "In Your Eyes" played as I opened the door. Closing it quietly, I tiptoed inside, hoping to get changed before he saw me.

A crash from the kitchen. Then laughter. I tugged my sweatshirt over my butt and crept to the entrance.

There was Francis: against the counter, head tilted back, his eyes closed. Gale stood against him, one leg wedged between my brother's thighs. He pushed his hands into my brother's hair and kissed his neck.

I gasped, and another cramp dragged through the core of me like an old rope.

The song ended. The music turned to the ominous strains of "Mercy Street." Francis opened his eyes to me in the doorway.

"What are you doing?" I said. It came out as a squeal. Like screaming tires.

I ran.

In my bedroom, I covered my face with my hands as Gabriel's rough-throated lullaby came through my door. *Dreaming of Mercy Street . . . In your daddy's arms again.*

Outside my door, I heard murmurs. The front door opened and closed. Click. Just like that: Goodbye, Gale.

Back against the wall, I slid to the floor. Just a bloody, foul girl.

SEVEN

Ben

"Why don't we talk about yesterday's group session?" Dr. Lambert says. "What sort of feelings came up for you?"

Gut feelings, sinking feelings, hooked on a feeling. Everyone is squirming on the end of a hook because nobody wants to meet the mouth. But it's coming. No one's getting out of this world alive.

Lambert shifts in his chair. "Which would suggest you see yourself as some kind of bait."

What could you catch with that kind of bait? Catch hell, catch your death. Fish or cut bait. Before you know it, you're swallowed whole, in the belly of the whale.

Lambert breathes. He folds his hands on his notes. Lambert's a waiter. He can wait all goddamn day.

A shout from outside the door cuts the quiet, down the hall, down the ward, down, down into the void. Anywhere but here. Or there. Find a way to nowhere. That's all Ben ever wanted. A road to nowhere.

There used to be a church bus that came through the old neighborhood, picking up kids for Sunday school. When the old man heard about it, he sent Ben and Cola curbside, so he could have his hangover to himself.

Know the story of Jonah and the Whale? Ben and Cola learned that one early on. They sat in a church basement and colored a whale and two Jonahs. They slit the whale's mouth so the paper Jonah doll could fit inside. The nuns gave them play-along story instructions: Stick the scared Jonah in the whale's mouth when he's being swallowed, and have the happy Jonah come out of his mouth when the whale spits him out.

Truth is: A happy Jonah is a gone Jonah. All Jonah wanted to get was gone. He wanted to get the hell away from God. That's the story.

The only place to truly get gone is the belly of the whale. Straight down the blowhole. The black hole. Away, away in the whale, that's all anyone wants. Until you get there. It's the stench that opens your eyes: the tin cans, the sardines, the old pizza boxes.

A full minute goes by before Lambert says, "I guess it was up to you to clean your father's apartment."

It had to be you, wonderful you. Ben's a doer. That's his job: to clean up the old man's mess. Everyone's mess. Everyone's except his own.

The old man was still shipwrecked, thrashing around like a fish full of feeling.

They slit his belly open and he fought. They pinned him to

the bed and still he fought. Strangely agile, the nurses said, for a guy who'd just been gutted.

He kept fighting and he kept bleeding. He bled so hard they shipped him to intensive care. Intense. Intents. For all intents and porpoises. That's where he lay, incised and dissected, eyes coasting across the ceiling as if he were searching the horizon for a way out.

A bag of blood dripped into his arm and all around him, tubes and monitors beeped and groaned, pissed and moaned because dear old Dad's own blood kept flowing like a river out to sea.

There you go, old man. This bed's for you. You made it; lie in it.

In intensive care every bed's got its own nurse. The name tag on the old man's nurse said ABBY C.

"He was wild about thirty minutes ago," Abby C said. "I had to give him Seroquel. It's an antipsychotic." Abby C had butterflies on her scrubs and a face like granite.

Cola stared at Ben, like Ben should bust her, show her who's boss. Forget it, kid. If Abby wants him, she can have him. Let the games begin.

Cola pulled the curtain around the cubicle to block out the world. He went bedside and gripped the side rails. "Hey, Dad." The old man's eyes rolled toward him, little black balls of fear, just like Cola's.

Cola took his hand. He said to Ben, "They're killing him. He's not even there."

True. The old man wasn't there. Maybe he went on a whaling expedition. Maybe he was haunting the doorway to limbo. Get in there, old man, it's your last hope.

"What if this is the new normal? What if he can't go back home?" Cola said. "Maybe we really do have to put him in a facility. Like Vera said."

Ben looked away. "Maybe he'll do us all a favor and die."

AT THE OLD man's apartment, an eviction notice was taped to the door. Imagine, kicking someone out of his own ruin, just like that.

Ben snatched the notice and opened the door.

The stench-everlasting, as if everything they ripped from the old man's guts was waiting right here, rotting and rejoicing.

For chrissake, open the sliding glass door. Open the window.

Cola rolled the balcony door open to the mountain of trash bags while Ben dialed the number on the eviction notice.

"It's protocol," said Maria, the manager. "If he pays his rent, he can toss the notice."

Ben said thank you like he meant it. "We'll clean. He needs a new carpet."

"Carpet?" Maria sounded pissed. She sounded like the old man was so close to gone she could taste it. "I need a mask in that place!"

Ben looked down at the bits of sea life and scraps stuck to the floor. "He's in the hospital." Ben's voice was flat as an afterthought when he added, "He's had surgery and he's hemorrhaging."

For a few seconds there was calm, like surf lapping the shore. "I'm the one who found him," Maria said. "I called the ambulance. He said he didn't have family."

Would that it were so, Maria.

You can't say that, though. You can't say, *Smooth move, Maria, why didn't you mind your own business?* Ben had to swallow it. Had to swallow all the sardine cans and broken bottles, and throw around some gratitude. "Thank you. I don't know why he'd say that."

Her pause sounded like You're-Not-Welcome. She'd request the carpet, she said. "And paint. I hope your father will be okay."

Ave Maria. Pray for us sinners, now and in the hour of our death. Ben spit up another thank-you and put the phone down.

He closed his eyes for a second and it felt something like peace. When he opened them he saw nothing but the same bottomless pit. On the balcony, flies buzzed from one trash bag to the next. They rubbed their hands together, ricocheted off the balcony into the room.

He slapped one from his temple as if it had teeth. "Let's get it in gear. I got to be at work in a couple hours."

IN THE ELEVATOR, one stinking bag in each hand, Ben watched the numbers light as the car creaked down the shaft.

There was a clatter on the floor as a lone pill bottle rolled between Cola's feet. "Shit," he said. "Bag's ripped."

The car stopped in the bowels of the building and the doors opened. Ben stepped out and Cola straggled, dropped one bag, and scrambled for the pill bottle.

"Leave it," Ben said.

Cola looked up from the floor. He pocketed the bottle as he stared at Ben in fluorescent light. "Have you looked in a mirror lately? Seriously, dude, you're turning green. You're going to drop dead if you keep going like this."

Cola doesn't know how hard it is to drop dead.

They threw the bags in the Dumpster and headed back for more.

Inside the elevator, Ben leaned, closed his eyes, and asked, "You pay back that money yet?"

"I called the guy. He knows I'm on it."

"Bet he loved that."

"He just wants his money," Cola said. "I'd bust heads too if someone owed me ten grand."

"It's ten now? Interest. Right." The doors opened and Ben's eyelids opened with them. "Don't be an asshole, Cola. Just go to the cops."

Cola followed Ben down the hall and through their father's door. "Then what? I'd be nobody. No one'd work with me again."

Ben stood in the middle of the apartment. He stared at the flies as they circled and landed, circled and landed. "You're already nobody."

Cola shoved past him onto the balcony, dug through the flies, and hauled four bags inside.

Ben watched him drag the bags, two in each hand, across the carpet. "They're going to rip, Cola, and then we'll be—"

"Fuck you, Ben."

Ben grabbed four bags and followed.

As the elevator dropped, Ben looked at Cola. *I'd bust heads too*—like he could sympathize. Cola thinks like a fly: Just keep moving and cling to the stink. "Does Vera know what's going on?"

"It's my business." Cola kicked his way out of the elevator and dragged his four bags across the cement, leaving a trail of slime and debris.

It was six o'clock in the evening by the time they got the last bag out. Ben's eyes kept sliding shut and his evening had not yet begun. Still had to drive a limo full of drunks on a downtown club crawl.

He went into his old man's cupboard and found a jar of Nescafé. Rinsing out a chipped teacup, he dumped in three tablespoons of instant coffee and turned on the hot water tap.

Cola leaned in the entrance to the kitchen. "Are we going to pay Dad's rent or what?"

Ben stirred the tarry sludge and then downed it. He tossed the cup in the sink, where it busted in two. Hand on his stomach, he looked into the sink and watched caffeine bleed off the jagged edges. Felt like an omen, like something was busted inside him too. Maybe it was just sardine cans and broken bottles rattling around in the bottom of his belly. His for life now.

"Are we going to pay it or not?" Cola said. Loud.

Ben turned a pair of dead eyes on his baby brother. Cola kept going: "He could pay you back when he's out. He's got money." But it all sounded like so many seagulls trailing him, screaming in the wind, waiting for him to fall and break open, all that muck and stench laid bare and inviting.

He shoved past Cola and riffled through old envelopes and bills strewn on the table until he found the old man's checkbook.

Ben sat down and wrote the date on the first check.

"What are you doing?" Cola said. Like another goddamn demand. It cracked Ben's skull, like lightning cracks a ship.

Ben printed the name of the company that owned his father's building on the payee line. He printed *Four hundred and twenty dollars and xx/100*, and then put himself in his old man's shoes, set pen to signature line, and scrawled like a sonuvabitch.

Cola hovered. "Can you do that? What if—"

What if, what if. What if the old man gave a shit? Ben ripped out a second check, made it out to Cola. *One thousand dollars and xx/100.* "Here, go buy yourself some time before they break your legs."

SEVEN

Maggie

I came across your name on the Internet," Lucy says. "In the news, I mean." She fidgets with her paper napkin. "I guess I went looking for it."

I nod and poke a fork at my *Numero Cinco: Chicken enchilada.*

We're sitting in a booth at Las Margaritas, a Mexican place near Lucy's apartment. She called early this afternoon and asked if I would take her car in for an oil change before I brought it back. She called again as I sat in the Jiffy Lube waiting room. She was feeling cooped up—"How about we get dinner together?" She called a third time to let me know that entrees are two-for-one if you order before 5:30 P.M.

The fourth call was to ask if I would be free for a game of Scrabble afterward.

"Awful thing to lose a child that way. Two and a half years old?" She shakes her head in sympathy. "It said that he, ah, your little boy got himself out of bed at night, and climbed up on the windowsill." She ducks her head, trying to catch my eye. "You don't blame yourself, do you?"

I don't want to talk about this with her.

"Well, you shouldn't. They're quick as lightning at that age. And another thing you shouldn't forget: Death is just a transition. Souls choose when to leave and I firmly believe—"

"How is your chicken flauta?"

Lucy looks at her plate. "Good." She clears her throat and then pounds her palm against her chest to clear her windpipes further. "Excuse me." After looking at me for a moment, she says, "I'm going to be eighty-one years old soon; I have learned a few things. Lloyd always said that I was more than just beautiful. I don't get to hear that very much, these days. Except last week, at the supermarket. I had asked a young fella for help reading a label. I told him I had trouble with my eyes and he said, 'You have *gorgeous* eyes!' I said, '*Me?*' And I had to get right up close to him because up close I can see perfectly and I said, 'Wow, you're pretty cute yourself,' and he said, 'Stand back, honey! I know that old trick.' Ha-ha!"

"That sounds fun," I tell her and take a bite of my enchilada.

"I came home and looked in the mirror and thought, Look at me! I have gorgeous eyes!" Lucy grins across the table. She glances at a middle-aged man in a suit, one table over. He appears very focused on what his dinner companion is saying.

"I love that tie!" Lucy shouts and leans out toward him. "I can't see. Is it paisley?"

Mouth full of food, he glances at his lady friend and back at Lucy. His friend looks vaguely annoyed at the interruption. "Yes," she says, then her face softens and she smiles at the tie. "I picked it out."

"Good taste!" Lucy crows. "I always tell people if something about them looks nice, because if you don't, the compliment goes to waste."

"True," says the woman with a laugh.

"How are you enjoying your meals, ladies?" Our server. She's got a worried round face. Her long, shaggy bangs don't quite cover the creases between her brows. I wonder if my eyes look as sad to her as hers do to me.

"Good," Lucy says. She pauses to watch the waitress head back to the service station. "She's got a big backside on her, doesn't she?"

Jesus, what's with the comments! And Lucy doesn't lower her voice when she makes them either. I put a hand over my mouth in hopes she might get the hint.

"You've got a cute bum," she blurts to me. "I noticed the other night what a neat little bum you have."

"Thanks."

"You're welcome. I always tell people if I think something about them looks nice. Because if you don't—Oh I just said that, didn't I? But it's true. People tell me I make their day!"

"I bet you do." I try to keep my tone light. I told Francis I likely wouldn't get back till nine or ten. Right now, all I want to do is go home. I wonder if I'm beginning to display agoraphobic tendencies.

"Are you free tomorrow afternoon?" Lucy asks. "Tomorrow's my birthday. I was hoping you could drive me somewhere."

"Tomorrow's your birthday? Eighty-one! Um, sure, where do you want to go?"

"There's a special Greetings from Spirit over at the, ah, the whatsits—There's a tea group that meets once a month at four. I just—I felt like I missed out the other night and I thought it would be nice to hear from Lloyd on my birthday."

"Is that medium you like going to be there? Monica something?"

"Monique Fontaine? No. It's just a little tea group. I thought it would be something fun to do."

Oaxacan folk art sits on a nearby shelf, all purples, yellows, and blues, dotted wings and striped quills. "I worry about you spending so much money on me as a chauffeur. You don't want me to vacuum or something? Do your dishes?"

"Don't be silly. I know what I need. And I have money. I think we make a good team, you and I. Who's that rich guy who used to say, 'You don't get paid for the hour, you get paid for the value you bring to the hour'?" She looks at me until I nod. "Anyway, I felt a little gypped when I didn't hear from Lloyd the other night. You in?"

Looking at the shelf of demented beasts again, I think of Frankie, and how he'd have climbed the walls to get his hands on those things. The thought brings a memory of the United Church of Spiritualism and Frankie ghosting in my lap. Recalling the sense of him is like rolling in warm cotton.

What does it matter if it's all a delusion? If I could spend all day in that dream, I would. "Sure, okay."

Lucy gives me a wink and digs into her flauta.

"How many times have you heard from Lloyd?"

"I bawled my eyes out the first time. I could always feel

him near but the first time I heard from him—Oh!" She puts a small, blue-veined hand to her heart. "Lloyd believed in the afterlife. He wasn't so much afraid of death as he was of ending up on life support, and I swore I'd never do that to him. So when he collapsed in the living room that night, the ambulance came and they started taking out their gizmos like they were going to try and resuscitate him and I said, 'Don't bother with that. He's dead. I didn't call you till I knew he was dead.'"

My mouth hangs. She what? What is she saying?

In my head now is a picture of Lloyd on the rug, shuddering with pain, unable to speak, and Lucy in their kitchen, filling the kettle, chattering away.

When Lucy finishes her main course, she pulls her purse into her lap and tugs on a stretchy silver cord attached to the lining with a safety pin until she gets hold of the magnifying glass at its end. She uses it to pore over the dessert menu. "Oh, I don't know. I think I'm too tired for Scrabble," she says and closes the menu. "Would you mind just dropping me off and calling it a night?"

She dumps the magnifier back in her purse and pulls on a gold cord until she gets hold of an old leather glasses pouch. Digging two fingers in, she ferrets out a stack of credit cards and ID. "Could you catch her eye and ask for the bill?"

ON THE DRIVE home, Lucy asks what time it is. When I tell her, she says, "Seven's not very late but I'm ready to get into my cozy bed." She looks over at me. "You must be tired too. You had to spend all that time with the oil change."

"Yeah, I'm ready for my PJs too."

As I turn onto her street, she says, "Just pull up front. You go ahead and take the car."

I want to say no. Keeping Lucy's car seems like a kind of hostage taking. Except I'm the hostage. But I can't say that and I feel like an ingrate for thinking it. "Lucy, I can't keep taking your car. It's—"

"You'll need it tomorrow. Why take the bus all the way— Where the hell did I put that?" She's rummaging in her purse. She pulls out a billfold attached to yet another stretchy cord. "Here we go." She hands me two fifty-dollar bills. "For the oil change and your time. The value you bring to your time!" She grins and puts her hand on the door handle. "Who's that?" She looks up at the entrance of her building. "Can you see—is that a woman?"

"Looks like it." I jump out, haul her walker out of the trunk, and wheel it over to the passenger side as I watch the woman key the handicapped entry. Both doors open wide for her. "It's a lady on a scooter. Blond hair, kind of heavyset, probably in her sixties."

"Oh her." Lucy puts her hands on the walker and hoists herself up. "Odette, that big, fat slob. She's so judgmental."

I check Lucy's face for a smile, some hint that she's in on her own absurdity. Nope. She's busy shaking her head, scowling at the very thought of Odette, that big-fat-slob of a judger.

ON THE WAY home, my cell rings. Lucy. I pull over. Maybe she left something in the car.

"Just wondering if the gas is getting low. Maybe you could put a few bucks in and I'll pay you back."

The fuel gauge is at three-quarters. "Okay. I'm on the road

now, so we better hang up and I'll see you tomorrow at three-thirty."

Not two blocks go by before the phone rings again. I hit SPEAKER and keep going. "Hey, Lucy."

"I hope you weren't insulted that I didn't feel like playing Scrabble. If you're keen, I could probably keep going for an hour or so."

"I'm pretty bushed. I'll take a rain check."

"Okey-dokey, then, dear. Oh by the way, do you like the color blue? Because I have a pretty blue scarf that I never wear. I've also got these tubes of conditioner that come with my hair dye. Would you be able to use—"

"Oh Lucy, there's a roadblock ahead. Better hang up. Talk tomorrow, okay!" I end the call.

I don't remember feeling this kind of impatience with Mary or Cecily or any of the others who used to employ me. What if I'm turning into an irritable asshole? What if this is all part of my transition to misanthropic hermit?

Coming upstairs to my apartment feels like deliverance. I just want to close my eyes and think of nothing.

Key in hand, I hear music on the other side, disco beat, techno music.

I open the door to find the living room deserted, but for some clothing on the couch and a nearly dry fifth of vodka on the coffee table. Two glasses.

On television, a young woman is popping her barely clad butt while singing in a voice so heavily pitch-corrected by AutoTune that she sounds like a robotic goat.

"Francis!"

I switch off the TV.

"Hey, baby!"

Baby? Who the hell is that? I stare at the half-closed door of my room. I walk over and push it open.

A man is on my bed. A very young man in a pair of jeans and nothing else. He looks up from the magazine he's reading—the magazine I left on my nightstand this morning.

"Oh! I thought you were Frankie," he says. "You must be his sister. He went, um, he went to get cigarettes."

Frankie? He speaks with the lazy bounce of a high school girl. "Who are you?"

"I'm Tyler." He looks down and turns a page. Tyler is lying on his stomach. Dingy blue-black barbed wire is tattooed around his slim right bicep.

"Why are you on my bed?"

"Is this yours? I thought it was um—" He rolls over, sits up, and dumps his feet on the floor. He looks me up and down with sleepy, drunk eyes. "You want a drink? I could do you a Purple Jesus. Grape juice and vodka."

The front door opens. I turn to face my brother.

"You're home," he says. "Early." Cigarette in his mouth, he squints through the smoke as he crams the keys back into the front pocket of his jeans.

"Where the hell were you?"

"Miss Congeniality . . ." His eyes look as slurred as his speech. "Did Tyler leave?"

"Who is Tyler? And what the fuck is he doing in my bed?"

"Tyler?" Francis pushes past me just as his friend comes out of my bedroom.

"Hey, Frankie." Tyler grabs his shirt off the sofa. He pulls it on and fumbles with two or three buttons.

"Where you going?" Francis says. He watches Tyler pull on his socks.

I step back against the wall by the front door and watch. I'd be surprised if this kid is even twenty.

Tyler's voice is lighthearted when he says, "I'm going to split, man."

"Because of *her*? Don't pay attention to *her* . . ." Arm limp at his side, Francis's cigarette dangles between two slack fingers. The lengthening ash drops to the floor as he watches Tyler step into his shoes. "Don't—you don't hafta—you want to go somewhere? Let's go to a club."

Tyler heads for the door, but Francis intercepts him.

"I'm wiped." Tyler takes my brother's chin between his thumb and forefinger and kisses him on the lips. "You're sweet. I'll catch you later."

"Oh no you don't, Tallulah." Francis grabs Tyler's wrist and weaves with the effort. "I'm coming with you."

"Just heading home to chill. Okay, man?" Tyler's smile has a plastic quality.

Francis shakes his head. "No, no, none of that." He looks around him and pats his pockets with his free hand. "I just gotta get my cigarettes."

"Seriously. I'm going home."

"Oh *pullease!*" My brother closes his eyes and opens them as if he can't quite focus. "Come off it. We have a whole night ahead of us."

Tyler tries to pull away but Francis holds tight. Tyler glances at me. He looks down at the hand on his wrist and his face turns hard. "Dude, I'm done. I'm leaving—you're staying. Get it?" He jerks free.

"Fine. Fuck off then, you little shit." Francis takes a quick, dramatic puff off his cigarette. "Don't come sniveling back to me when you want your cock sucked."

Tyler snorts, opens the door, and slams it behind him.

Still against the wall, I let my breath go. "You bring some kid home and—and fuck him in my bed? What is wrong with you? What—"

I don't even have the words. Who are we anyway?

Another chunk of ash falls from his cigarette as he raises it to his lips. "What's wrong with *me*? *You* can't stand to see me happy. You had a shit fit the first time you found me with a guy and nothing's changed. I'm a fag, Maggie. Suck it up."

"Are you nuts? I don't give a crap who you fuck. But your bishop probably does."

"My bishop. He's too busy getting his own blow jobs, but *you*—I looked after you, I took care of you, and all I ever got was, was, homophobic, jealous, angry . . ."

"You're drunk, Francis."

"Yeah? And you're . . . a dried-out, miserable old bitch." His eyes have never looked so full of disgust.

Here come the tears. Christ. I don't want to give him the satisfaction.

I cross my arms. "I think you should leave."

He laughs and nods and then shakes his head. "You think I don't have pain? You think you're the only one? Goddamn Vatican sends their minions around to root out the homos . . . and then I get it from my own sister!"

Francis studies the nub of his cigarette and looks around

himself, presumably for some place to put it out. When he can't find anything, he looks at me, holds his hand up, and then grinds the burning cherry into his palm.

"We can both go to hell," he says, then drops the butt in his shirt pocket and walks out the door.

EIGHT

Ben

S ounds as if the days leading up to your hospitalization were spent looking after a father who didn't do much fathering," Lambert says.

Here he goes again with the father shit. Father this, father that. Digging in the dirt and making mud pies.

"But you kept showing up," he says. "Must have been difficult to bite your tongue."

Bite your tongue. Bite the dust. All your enemies with their mouths open against you. Ben's the kind of dupe who gives them more teeth to do the job right. Even the old man, lying there toothless and diapered: perfect place to leave him. Not old Ben. He keeps showing up like a kicked dog. Circling, waiting.

Those chill pills, those antipsychotics they gave his old man, they made him seem almost human. Wrists still tied, but he was talking, not trying so hard to rip out the tubes.

Ben showed up with his dentures. Maybe the nurses could

put them in and the old man would start to look human too.

"Wondered where the hell those were," the old man said. Hard to make out when he's all gums. "Can 'ou shash my nose?"

You scratch my nose, I'll scratch yours. Never works out that way, does it?

Ben stared at the old man's sunken eyes, his sunken lips. He reached past the bed rail and rubbed his father's nose. The old man moved his head around like a cat, and looked at Ben as if he loved him.

Ben pulled back, stuck his hands in his pockets.

"Can you get these things off me?" The ties on his wrists. Fit to be tied. Even with one hand tied behind his back.

"No. I can't."

A nurse came to the foot of the bed. "Are you his son?" She told Ben they'd had to give the old man another unit of blood. Pressure kept dropping. Had to send him down for another scope and an MRI. "You can untie one of his hands if you want. Just make sure you tie it back up before you go. He's fast!" She went back to the monitor at her desk.

Fast and furious. When he was a kid, Ben heard a story about Willie Nelson and what a miserable prick he was when he drank. His wife waited until he passed out one night, tied him up with the kids' jump ropes, and then beat him black and blue. Why didn't Miriam do that? Why don't we do that?

He looked away. "I gotta take off."

"My teeth?"

Who's afraid of the big bad wolf? Ben looked at the denture container. "You want me to get the nurse?"

The old man shook his head.

Ben opened the box, took out the upper. His old man stared up with the trust of a lamb. He opened his sad mouth as if he was about to receive Communion.

Ben slipped it in, watched him try to push it in place with his tongue. The teeth flopped around his mouth. Christ. Ben untied the nearest wrist, unwound the long cotton strap.

The old man's eyes teared up. He raised his freed hand as if he wanted to touch Ben's face.

Forget it. Ben's had enough of that hand.

The old man brought the shaking thumb to his mouth instead, pressed the upper to his gum.

"Ready for the bottoms?"

He opened his mouth again, looked up at Ben. Looked at him like Cola. Baby Cola and his bottle. Round brown eyes staring up like worship. Like he would love him forever.

Both sets in his head now, the old man clacked his dentures together and winced. "Hurts," he said.

"I better get going," Ben told him. "We're cleaning your place. Me and Cola. Getting a new carpet." He retied the old man's free wrist.

"My place?" Like he wasn't sure what the words meant.

"Your apartment."

"My apartment . ... in Ireland?"

Ireland? Maybe Cola was right. Maybe his mind went with that chunk of colon.

"Your apartment here. On Jackson Avenue."

"Jackson," he repeated. His fingers groped at the side rail, trembling, looking for a hand to hold.

Put your hand in the hand. All hands on deck.

He searched Ben's face and said, "I'm scared."

Ben stared at the knot of fingers against the sheet. "I'm scared" bored into his head, rushed up and down until it found his heart and piled on. His tongue roamed around in his mouth, hunting for words. A faraway voice whispered, "Me too," but nothing came out.

A HALF HOUR later and there's Ben on the sidewalk out front of the old man's building. He checks his watch. Fucking Cola. Ben went through the online classifieds after work this morning, looking for someone who could do laundry and scrub the bathroom while he and Cola hacked away at the rest of the place.

He checks his phone and hits redial.

"Hey!" Cola says. "What's up?"

"Where the hell are you?"

Cola's voice lowers. "I got something going on."

"Are you shitting me? We have to drag all his crap into the hall so they can rip up the carpet tomorrow. They're painting tonight!"

"Come on, man. Anyone can do that. I gotta be here. This is going to save my bacon."

"You little prick. And what about that thousand bucks I gave you? Did you talk to the guy—"

A woman pulls up to the curb in an old junker. She jumps out. "Are you Ben?"

He hangs up on Cola. "Janet?" He swallows. The sight of her hauling that bag of cleansers and rags, like the old days: dropping Maggie out front of some old lady's apartment, kissing her goodbye, Frankie in the backseat.

He offers to take Janet's bag.

In the elevator, he stares at the floor. Looks nothing like Maggie. She's got a brassy yellow mullet, bangs teased up over her forehead, the back tied with elastic.

Ben fidgets. Elevator feels like it's closing in. "My brother was supposed to be here but he pulled a Houdini on me."

She chews her thumbnail. "Guess he didn't feel like workin' today."

The doors open and Ben's out in a shot. He sucks the hall air with relief.

Then reality starts to push in. Now he's got to be alone with her in the old man's pigsty.

"You'll have to forgive the smell," he says. "It's like something died in here. I mean—nothing did. My dad's sick. He's in the hospital."

When he opens the door, the stink hits like humiliation. Ben makes a dash for the balcony and opens the sliding glass door all the way.

She takes it all in, pokes her head into the bathroom. "I've seen worse."

Her eyes are worried and hard at once. Her skin is weathered into deep creases around her nose and mouth. Who does she remind him of?

At least the tins are off the floor, sour milk and cereal off the nightstand. "You wanna start with the laundry? This first bag is all towels and sheets. I'd go with the hot water setting."

She looks in the closest green garbage bag. "And bleach," she says.

He hands her a roll of quarters. "Ground floor, left of the elevators. Maybe I should carry—"

"I'm fine." She shoves the quarters into her back pocket.

"Can you stay late? Until we're done, I mean."

She shakes her head. "I have to pick up my son at four thirty." She hoists the laundry and soap, walks out the door.

He watches her disappear down the hall. Ben's no good with strangers anymore. It's different when he's working. He's in the driver's seat.

Once Janet has three loads going, she pulls on a pair of yellow rubber gloves and starts in on the bathroom.

Ben faces the old man's stripped bed and listens to Janet clunk around the tub.

He drags the mattress off and grapples it onto its side. Glancing at the box spring, he blinks: cash scattered like more trash. A quick glance over his shoulder and Ben picks up the bills: a hundred and eighty bucks. He stares at it until his eyes glaze, until he sees that knot of fingers again, against the white sheet. His fingers tingle with the sensation of tying down his old man before leaving the hospital. Should have felt good doing that. Should have felt sweet.

He folds the cash and crams it into his back pocket.

Wrestling the old man's mattress, he drives it across the room and shoves it through the front door. Leaning it in the hall, he rests on it, catches a breath. Feels like he's got an anvil tied to his ass. Every day it gets a little heavier. Should go down to the high school and see if some kid wants to make fifty bucks. Two guys could clear this place in half an hour.

Going back for more, he pauses at the bathroom door. Janet's on the floor, bent over the tub, scouring. The sight of her on her hands and knees hurts his guts. He's paying her fifteen bucks an hour, but it still looks wrong. She hops into the tub and catches him watching.

She looks at her feet. "Should I take off my shoes? They're sneakers. I—"

"No. I was just wondering if you had a husband who might want to make a few bucks. Help me move this stuff into the hall."

The word *husband* bites like teeth.

"No." She sprays the tiles with some kind of foam and scrubs.

Ben wipes an arm across his face and goes back to the bed. Fucking Cola.

He pulls the box spring from the wall and flips it on its side. On the carpet: a blue-furred half sandwich, bits of chips and pretzels, and an open bottle of cough syrup stuck to its own green ooze. Need a rake to make a dent in this dump. He tosses bottles into a garbage bag until he discovers one with a lone blue tablet inside: *clonazepam*, 1 mg. Cola's voice echoes: "Seriously, dude, get some sleeping pills." He tilts it, watches it slide around the bottle, and then crams it into his pocket with the cash.

At four o'clock, Janet shucks her rubber gloves and starts packing up. Layers of kitchen crud have disappeared. The bathroom shines like a Tonka toy.

Ben watches her pull her sweater on. "You, ah—great job."

"You look really tired," she says.

Ben stares at her stiff blond bangs and his brain stews in déjà vu. "So, fifteen an hour, right? That's ah . . ."

"We went through this when my grandpa got sick," Janet says. "Nobody got hardly any sleep." She looks at her hands and then at him again. "Seventy-five dollars."

Ben glances in at the sparkling toilet and it hits him: the

echo of stadium bathrooms, the cool of a porcelain sink against the back of his head, watching her scrub out toilet after urinal—Miriam's thin blond hair.

"Right." He reaches into his back pocket and takes out the old man's wad. He counts off four twenties, and then hears that shadow voice like ground glass: "I don't clean other people's shit. That's your line."

There's a wisp of fear in her face. *I don't clean other people's . . .* Did he think that or did he say it? Heat rushes up his neck. Feels as if his head is being squeezed. Like a crown of razor wire, tighter and tighter.

He pushes the whole hundred and eighty at her. Just take it.

She looks at the cash. "That's too much."

He shows her the door. "Go pick up your son. Before he falls and hurts himself."

She gathers up her supplies, fumbling with the mop and pail.

He puts his hand on her back and the sense of her—her motherness—rushes up his arm. Don't go. Please don't go. Like he's going to grasp at her coattails, and sob at her feet.

No. She's the one who should cry. Not Ben.

Get out. And out and out. Here's five bucks. Go get yourself a burger.

Janet's mouth trembles.

Good. Cry. *I'm scared.* Be scared, the two of you. Two peas, two of a kind. Don't need you. Don't need anybody. He shoves her into the hall, walls lined with the old man's furniture. Go be in charge of someone else's misery. He slams the door.

Facing the half-empty room, he squeezes his eyes shut. What did he just say? What did he think and what did he say?

A knock at the door. He turns. She called the cops?

The knob turns. Ben snatches the door open: Cola. Vera right behind him.

"Whoa!" Cola says. He puts his hands up. "Don't shoot. Ha-ha!"

Ben looks at them until the fog clears. "Look who's here. Day late and a dollar short."

"Least we're here," Cola says. He's chipper. "Vera got to leave early today cuz she works late tomorrow."

Vera muscles in a little closer and puts her hands on her hips. "We're here to help. How about a little civility?"

"It's okay," Cola says.

"No. It's not." She keeps her guard dog glare on Ben. "Cola is not your whipping boy."

"Let it go, Vera." Cola puts his hand on her arm.

She shrugs him off. "You're an asshole, Ben—and yet Cola keeps on loving you." She snorts at the absurdity.

Creeping in the back of Ben's brain are FuckYou and GoToHell, but they're too far away and too much effort to get out.

He looks at Cola. "You wanna give me a hand with the dresser?"

The two of them hump it toward the front door while Vera pokes around the apartment, assessing.

"Sorry about today," Cola whispers, once they have the dresser in the hall. "I went with Vera to work. They have these 'shadow days' where people can come and follow the vets and techs around."

Ben grunts with the effort of keeping the dresser moving.

"Vera's clinic is the central branch. She's in charge of ordering for all four clinics." He scoots around to push from Ben's side. "Vera's a big deal down there." He turns his lost eyes on Ben. "I know you don't like her, but she likes me."

WHEN BEN GETS home, he pulls the old man's pill bottle from his pocket. He shakes it, listens to the harsh rattle of one lone pill against plastic. Take as needed, the label says.

He stares at the old man's name and thinks about Mrs. Cecily G. Riley.

When's the last time he called the old girl? She should be kept informed, shouldn't she? He finds her number, hits REDIAL, and hangs up before the first ring.

He chucks the vial at the garbage, misses, and watches it roll across the carpet right back to him. Like it wants him. Wants to be wanted. It rolls under the couch and hunches there, waiting.

EIGHT

Maggie

It is 9:27 A.M. when my intercom sounds. I'm awake. I've been awake most of the night.

"Maggie?" It's Francis. His voice is pitched high and anxious. "Will you let me in? I, ah, I lost my key." I press the release to the house door, flip the lock on the suite door, then sit on the couch. My brother's heavy feet echo up the wooden staircase.

Francis slips inside and closes the door quickly, as though he's being chased. He blinks around the room. Catching his breath, he looks at the floor. He's wearing the shirt that he left in last night, but no jacket. "Sorry. I just, ah, I lost my keys and my cell phone and, ah, ah . . ." He closes his hand, winces, and opens it again to look at the cigarette burn in the center of his palm.

I don't nod, shake my head, or speak. Just sit there and let him spin.

"That reporter you ran into, Katie something?—she buzzed when you were out yesterday and I told her to get lost. She must have left and come back because she was out there again last night. I told her about rehab and . . . maybe other things." He looks at the blistered mess on his palm again. "She said she wanted to talk to me when I was sober, which is ridiculous because I was fine last night. Mostly. She wants to tell my story. Maybe it could help other people. I gave her my number and now I can't find my phone. Or my keys."

His hands are trembling and his face is covered in a sweaty sheen. He gulps more air and clamps his lips together.

Eventually he lifts his eyes to mine. "I'm sorry. Maggie, I'm really sorry."

It's hard to keep my voice low and even, but I do it. "Where did you go last night?"

"Um, well, I went to a bar looking for some ice." He turns his blistered palm to me. "And who do I see, but Tyler—the lying little shit—and we, ah, got into it a bit and then I left with some guys I met. We went to another bar so I could get some more ice for my hand and then, ah, home. To their place. Someone's place. I wish I had a cigarette." He looks around as if one might magically appear.

He pauses and his eyes turn red and watery. "I heard from Father Michael and the lawyer yesterday. I'm supposed to check in to Our Lady of Perpetual Help Rehab Center at the end of the week. For six months. Won't know about jail time until the trial. Which is ten days after I get out."

My voice comes in a croak. "Am I supposed to feel sorry for you?"

Francis chews his lips and blinks back tears. "I have a disease. I'm—"

"Oh shut up, Francis. And by the way, I have never come down on you for being gay. A shit fit? I was sixteen. As far as I was concerned, you stole my boyfriend, and yes, I'm perfectly aware that that was a fantasy on my part, but the fact still remains: If you'd come clean about who you were to start with, you could've saved us both a lot of pain."

He doesn't answer so I keep going. "Sixteen years later and nothing's changed except now you're an alcoholic priest. You're a *priest*! You break half your goddamn vows every day. It's your 'vocation'? Is that a disease too?"

"You think I don't wake up every day and recommit myself? *Today it stops*," he shouts then lowers his voice. "But I—I can't stop. I don't know how. I love God, but I love sex and men too. And booze."

I flop back against the couch and close my eyes. My cell phone vibrates on the coffee table. Reaching over, I check the call display. "Oh look, it's you." I answer.

"Is that Maggie? This is Katie Wilks from the *Herald*. We met a couple of days ago. I've got your brother's cell phone here."

"Clearly," I say, hit the speaker, and hold out the phone so that her voice fills the room.

"Has she got my wallet?" Francis whispers.

"I tried to call him this morning and some homeless guy answered. Apparently, he found Father Luke's phone sitting on a mailbox at Elm and First. I've also got a jacket, his wallet, and some keys. I gave the guy ten bucks and he turned it all over."

"Hi, Katie, it's me, Father Luke." Francis takes the phone from me. "Thank you so much! I don't know how to repay you."

"Sure you do!" She laughs brightly. "I'm actually downstairs right now. If you want to buzz me in, I can bring your stuff up."

Francis glances at me. "Actually, maybe I better just meet you out front."

BY THE TIME he comes back, I've got coffee going. My guts are still churning as I try to formulate a succinct question, something precise enough to open the box—the emotional tabernacle my brother is living in.

The two of us sit on the couch, clutching mugs of caffeine.

"She's going to ask you the same things I am, you know: You can't stop drinking and you can't stop fucking and yet your calling card says Celibate Priest. Why?"

Francis bites off a corner of buttered toast and ruminates. "I guess it's the old Oscar Wilde thing, *I can resist everything except temptation.*"

"Not that. Why the priesthood? Seems like it's *you* who feels shitty about you being gay, not me. Did you imagine that becoming a priest would make it go away?"

"No." My brother gives me a slightly exasperated look as though I should know better. "I wanted to be a priest long before I knew I was gay. And nobody ever said that sexual desire would go away. My vocational directors were pretty clear about that. I remember some eighty-year-old Jesuit saying, 'It'll go away when you're six feet under.' I'm just weak is all."

"So is Tyler your boyfriend? Is he even legal?"

"He's twenty-two. He's—we're not exclusive."

"Great. Good to know you're not tying yourself down to anyone. I noticed he called you *Frankie*."

"I guess I found it comforting."

I wish I hadn't brought that up. I want the focus to stay on Francis. I want him to answer for himself.

"I thought the rest of the world called you Father Luke. Or do you compartmentalize? I'm trying to understand, Francis, I really am." I watch him set his blistered palm on the side of his hot mug and then gasp and pull it away. "Why do you have to be a priest?"

"I've explained this to you. Many times. I want to help people. I wanted to be close to God. Since I was small . . ." He stares into his cup for a couple of moments. "Church always felt like the safest place to be. Those kids used to torment the shit out of me when I was little and the sisters would bring me inside and I loved it there. I loved them. You were too young. You don't remember."

"I do too." I remember.

Francis has a gentle nature, our mother used to say. She meant that he preferred soccer, which, in our neighborhood, was the girly alternative to football. She meant that he was very tidy and he was obsessed with his hair being just right before he would leave the house. And she meant that even though he was big for his age, the boys still managed to beat the crap out of him.

They called him faggot, homo, gayboy, poofter, queer, fudgepacker—I didn't know what the words meant, but I knew they were bad. I knew that a homo was the ultimate object of ridicule.

They pushed his face into dog shit. That I remember. I was in grade two, seven or eight years old. Francis would have been eleven or twelve. The three o'clock bell had rung a while back and I was late coming outside, straggling onto the blacktop out back of the school. Francis usually waited there for me, but he was gone and I was anxious.

I heard shouting in the distance, ran to the sidewalk, and saw them, half a block down: four boys shoving him up against the chain-link fence.

Sprinting toward them, I paused to snatch my brother's lunch box from where it lay on the sidewalk, just as Keith Boyle grabbed Francis by the back of the neck and forced him down to the ground. "Come on, say it, you little faggot, say 'I'm a shit-stabber.'" The ground was wet and Keith was pushing my brother's face toward a melting lump of dog dirt. "You must eat shit all the time, right, shit-stabber?"

I ran at them hard, swinging the lunchbox. Pete Duffy caught my arm and tossed me to the pavement.

I started to cry. My leotards were torn and my knee was bleeding. "You let him go or I'll fucking kill you. Fucking asshole."

A chorus of giggles.

"Whoa! Big talk." Duffy laughed.

Keith Boyle jammed his knee against my brother's back. "Do you practice on your sister? Is that why she's got such a dirty mouth?"

Scanning the street for a grown-up, I finally realized Good Shepherd was just on the other side of the road. I got up, bolted across the road, and up the stairs, slamming in through the front doors.

The smell of incense and the gentle quiet of the church silenced me for a moment. Sister Clare looked back from the front pew.

"Sister? They're going to kill him. You have to come."

We didn't go to church often, but Sister Clare knew Francis. She knew the neighborhood too; she jumped up and charged down the aisle, her twiggy legs pumping hard.

I chased after her and stopped on the bottom step of the church as she ran across the road toward the group of boys.

"You get away from him." She shook her fist as she went.

The boys stepped back. All except Keith Boyle, who stayed right where he was, pinning Francis to the ground. He shoved him by the neck and punched him in the back of the head.

"You stop it now, Keith Boyle. I mean it, you knock it off or so help me God, I'll shove your teeth down your throat." She grabbed Boyle by the hair and tried to pull him off.

I dashed across the road to get a better look.

"Don't touch me!" Boyle flailed and jumped up off the ground, panting and red-faced, and then slammed his fist into Sister Clare's stomach.

She doubled over. I gasped.

Silence. The other boys took another step back, their mouths open, waiting.

Keith Boyle stared at her. His eyes seemed to tremble in his head. He looked at Francis and wiped his hands on his jeans. My brother stayed where he was, facedown, curled into a ball.

Sister Clare took a breath and straightened up. Then she squared her wiry little body over her feet and delivered a punch that sent Boyle sprawling on his ass. He didn't move or speak at first. Then he lay back in the grass and stared up at the gray sky. Tears slid out the corners of his eyes.

There was a simpering giggle from the other boys.

Sister Clare let her gaze settle on each of them as she spoke. "I'll give your father a call, Mr. Boyle. Same goes for you, Mike Conner, Peter Duffy, Jason—I've got your numbers. I know where you live."

"Sorry, Sister," Duffy muttered. The three bystanders took a last look at Keith Boyle, jammed their hands in their pockets, and trudged away. Boyle rolled his head to the side and watched them go. His jaw was red and stormy where Sister Clare's punch had connected.

He climbed onto his feet and looked at us. For a moment it seemed he might say something, but he turned away, and trailed up the sidewalk after his friends.

"Okay, Francis, come on." Sister Clare crouched beside him. "Come inside and we'll get you cleaned up."

My brother's back heaved and shook. I knelt on the other side of him, laid my hand on the back of his head, and stroked him like a scared pet. "They're gone, Francis."

There was a small whimper from him when Sister Clare lifted his shoulders. The stink of dog shit was close and heavy. It was smeared across his mouth and nose, his hands. Tears streamed and he tried to cover his face.

Sister Clare grimaced. Once she had him on his feet, she draped her arm across his shoulders and walked him back toward Good Shepherd, pulling him tight to her side as they went. I picked up my brother's lunchbox and followed them up the stairs, concentrating on Sister's navy tunic, her sensible black shoes. I marveled at how tough she was, especially for someone so short and skinny and female. I wondered if there was such a thing as God-power.

While Sister Clare took my brother down the hall to get cleaned up, I waited in a pew and fidgeted with the hole in my tights. I stared up at the crucifix high on the wall. Light shone down on Christ's sad, dying face. So mean, I thought. Why do people have to be so mean?

"I KNOW WHAT they did to you," I tell Francis now. "You think I don't remember Keith Boyle?"

"One of many," Francis says. He gets off the couch and heads to the kitchen. "But those nuns were always there for me. Sister Clare, Sister Angelica. I used to go over there for Father Jim's noon mass. In grade two, I got an assignment to draw what I wanted to be when I grew up and I drew Father Jim." He comes back with the coffeepot and gives us each a top-up. "Church was the safest place in the world. The smell of it, the atmosphere—it felt like God. I wanted to feel that way all the time, like my relationship with God was the most natural thing in the world. Nothing made me feel that way like church." He stands over the coffee table, holding the pot. His gaze drifts as if he's considering his own words. "Then the Vatican started with their saber rattling—*We're going to root out the gays!* Sure as heck doesn't feel safe now."

"What do you like about it then?"

"I like being a priest."

An incredulous laugh escapes me. "*Why?* Is it the robes? Getting all dressed up in the vestments? Is it like the ultimate drag show or what?"

He snorts and carries the coffeepot back to the kitchen.

"It's a *drag* all right. But not the fun kind. Familiarity breeds contempt."

I listen to him putter, wipe the counter, and toss silverware in the sink. Eventually he says, "To get that feeling now, that close-to-God feeling, I have to find it around me, in people and in nature."

"Which brings us back to the original question," I call back. "Why do you stay in the church?"

Seconds go by. A minute. "Francis?"

"I heard you."

He drifts back into the living room and wanders to the window, coffee cup in his good hand. Parting the short sheers with his blistered hand, he rests his forehead against the pane. "I'm not going to jump ship just to pander to my own sexual stuff." His voice trails off as he says, "Every day I recommit. Every day I pray for help."

Watching his silhouette, I think of us when we were young. Francis used to tell me to pray. Ask for help, he'd say. I think I was about twenty when I turned on him and said, "Oh fuck off with your imaginary friend."

He'd looked at me with a pained expression. "Maggie, even if there's nothing out there, at the very least you might be waking up some sleepy part of your brain and putting it to work. You're acknowledging that you need help, and that's huge."

That's Francis. Over and over. No matter what, he finds a way to hope.

NINE

Ben

Every child deserves a parent, a foundation he can count on. That didn't happen for you." Dr. Lambert's at it again. He's got his pity face on. Poor Ben. Poor fucked-up Ben.

Don't feel sorry for Ben. He's long gone, kicking up sand, dreaming in the dirt, not a care in the world.

"Yet you showed up at his hospital bedside. Almost daily."

Almost daily day of reckoning. Blood will tell. Every day another son's hands on another windowpane, end over end, blood over blood.

Even the old man was somebody's bloody son. Who fucked him up?

"That's a good question and it brings us back to something we touched on the other day. Growing up with a man like your father, did you ever fear what kind of parent you would be?"

Ben was never going to be that old man. Head on Maggie's big belly, he promised. He told Frankie. Ben was waiting for Frankie since forever. Since the night that Miriam said, "Do you think I should go back to him?" As soon as Ben got away, there'd be no going back. He told Frankie. He told Maggie. Maggie was a believer. Not like Miriam. Maggie was a promise.

Back of a limo, the first time Ben saw Maggie. It was cold out, Christmas lights up and down the block, up and down the world. Maggie back there for a work party, a year-end gift from the company big shots. Free booze. Gallons—every set of teeth floating. Night over, the car tipped at the curb and they all poured out. All except Maggie. Left alone, alone to go home, only one sober. Home, James.

Ben watched her face in the rearview, got hooked on those sad eyes, neon light sparking around them, slow eyes, blue eyes, melancholy baby eyes, glinting behind gin bottles and stoplights. Like *Viva Las Vegas* next to the Sistine Chapel.

"Do you like Christmas?" That was Maggie.

"No," Ben said. Then he watched and waited. Maybe she loved Christmas. Maybe it soothed her like warm milk and mittens.

Maggie eyes floating in the mirror. Acid eyes, kaleidoscope eyes that tripped and burned and saw it all. "Christmas," she said. "People disappear and it all falls apart."

Maggie said that. Like she knew things. Ben in the driver's seat, hands on the wheel, but he was sucked straight down a rabbit hole, through a wormhole, a keyhole.

Say more, say more.

"I'm going to quit."

What'd she mean by that? Quit Christmas? Quit the world?

There were papers beside Ben. A client sheet. Something about research. Focus groups. Not those eyes, they pulled focus, switched focus. "What do you do?"

"I'm a fly on the wall."

Ben thought of the old man. Miriam. Dirty fly, he called her, touches shit all day, he said. That's all she's fit for. Better off without her, he said. Fly away, fly off the handle, straighten up and fly right.

What's it like to be a fly? "What's the worst thing about it?"

Quiet back there. A few three-hundred-pound seconds. None-of-your-business seconds? Shut-up-and-drive seconds?

"Desire is shaped by fear." She says it like a quote. Like she's been scaring people for years, making them want forever. "That's how you sell stuff," she says, and her face is like shame. She looks away.

Don't look away. Never look away. Ben might disappear when you look away.

She says, "What's the worst part of your job?"

"Vomit."

She snorts. The gilded Madonna snorts and fills the car with tinsel and solace and Ben says, "What's so funny?"

"At least it's real," she says. "Genuine puke."

Say more. Say Ben. Say puke. She feels like home. Feels like he had to drive ten thousand miles to find a girl from his own neighborhood.

"I think I'd rather clean up puke. At least I'd be helping. There are people who have no one." She stares out the window. "Old people . . . kids . . ."

Ben should've met her when *he* was a kid. Should have

found her on the sidewalk, playing jacks or hopscotch. Draw a chalk circle and stand in the middle. He'd have found her. He'd have saved her. She'd have saved him right back.

Through the miles and miles of dark he searches those eyes. He can see playgrounds and lightning. He can see his cradle and his grave, his mother and his child.

He can see the skylights open and the two of them drift up, into a heart-shaped future. He can see it. He knows it.

That's how it's going to be.

That's how it is.

When Maggie has Frankie, she has Ben. She gives birth to them both, hands against both sides of her belly, hands against the rising moon, on the inside and the outside. Maggie gives birth to the universe.

She gives birth to tiny fingers and peanut butter breath and toy cars and the weight of that boy lying on Ben's chest. Baby teeth spark a whole new Ben. Sponge ball in the park, kicking and running in circles till they drop. Frankie learns the staring contest. He loves it like he made it up. All eyes on deck, no blinking. Ben gets to stare into the universe and Frankie gets to look in Ben's attic, and his closets, deep in the back at the grime and dark and each time Frankie looks, he laughs a little harder. Fearless. Like a Buddha. Like it's safe. Like it couldn't hurt a fly. Who'd want to sleep when awake is so damn funny.

Enough to make you laugh right back. Enough to make you dance. Ben and Maggie dancing. Just the two of them, floating in the kitchen.

Ben took care of the rest. He believed in fearless. Just the two of them, floating in the kitchen. He loved her so hard, the attic disappeared and the closets and the flies. He loved them so much he didn't keep watch. And then suddenly it was yesterday—already past—like a watch in the night. The moon disappeared, the bed, and the mirrors and the mother and the child. All of it out the window. Even the window disappeared.

Who needs the old man when you've got Ben? Blood will tell.

NINE

Maggie

Standing at the window in my living room Francis says, "I'm going to go down and see Ben this afternoon."

What? What in God's name is he talking about?

"You just got in the door after—"

"—another royal fuckup. I know." He turns and sits on the sill. "I *need* to do this, Maggie."

"Is this some kind of atonement? If anyone should be down there it should be me."

Francis looks at me. I look into my hands.

AFTER FRANKIE DIED, I began to feel as though anyone I met must know at once that I was the most contemptible bit of filth he or she would ever lay eyes on. I felt as if I should be driven into the wilderness.

Francis tried to be pastoral at first, but coming from him it was insulting—all the God talk and the prayer. Couldn't he just shut up and be my brother? I hadn't been in a Catholic church since I was eighteen, when Francis announced that he would be leaving me for God.

But what do you do with death? Where do you go when you need someone to lift you out of the mire, forgive you, and rock you to sleep?

I snuck off to five o'clock mass at St. Clare's Cathedral on the outskirts of town. I didn't tell anyone, not Francis or Ben. Coming back into a church after all those years felt shameful somehow. I wore a shawl over my head—hid under it like a widow—and sat in the very back pew.

I watched a woman about my age praying in the same pew at the opposite end. A tiny smile played around her mouth; she looked so content, so free from doubt. I wanted that. I tried to pray, but all I could hear was my own voice echoing back. No matter how I genuflected, crossed myself, or rubbed at a rosary, I couldn't escape that terrible sense of dread that I was the ghost, not Frankie.

Over the next few weeks, I tried the Episcopalians, the Baptists, the Methodists, and the Pentecostals. I tried a synagogue. I tried a Buddhist temple. But there was nothing. Not for me. Not in a temple, and not at home.

When I finally told Ben what I'd been doing, it was a confession. We rarely spoke anymore and the sound of my voice in our apartment had a strange hollow quality. "I'm scared," I said. "I'm scared that I'll never be whole again."

Ben looked at me for a long time. Then he said those damning words of his: "How do you fill a hole?"

I gave up. I left.

WE PULL UP out front of St. Anthony General and I put Lucy's old Volvo in park. St. Anthony is the patron saint of lost things: seems particularly fitting right now.

The engine idles as I wait for Francis to make a move. The closer we got to Ben, the less we said. Now we sit in silence, catching our breath and fidgeting.

Francis had a hot shower before we left, and he's still damp. A slow, warm rivulet slides out of his hairline down his temple. He's sweating out last night's vodka, but I'm starting to wonder if fear is playing a part too.

It should be me going in there, but I can't calm the shudder in my chest. Knowing Ben's inside, on the brink of Here and Not-Here, makes my guts roil.

The night the police called me I sat beside Ben in the recovery room and watched him sleep, his head wrapped in bandages, monitors beeping. I kept looking at his hand, the pulse sensor on his index finger—did he pull the trigger with that finger? How could he do it? It was almost as if he'd shot us both. Slammed the door for good.

When I called the hospital the next day, they said he had stabilized. They had moved him to the psych ward.

"Are you sure about this?" I finally ask my brother.

"I should have been here days ago," Francis says.

"I don't know who you're going to find. He's supposed to be in a dissociative state. That's what they said."

"I can relate." His voice sounds odd. Something like surrender. As if his plan to make a pastoral visit to his brother-in-law in a psychiatric ward is a train that can't be stopped.

"Listen, I know Ben's never been able to make much sense

of me"—Francis touches the white plastic collar blaring out from his black clerical shirt—"but it's all I got."

"He actually does respect you, Francis . . . what you do."

My brother's eyebrows jump a little in disbelief, or relief, I'm not sure which.

The curbside sign says NO PARKING: PATIENT DROP-OFF AND PICKUP ONLY. I check the rearview to make sure no one is trying to shoo me away. Looking past Francis into the main lobby of the hospital, I can see patients and family milling near the admitting desk, asking questions, being discharged. Ben didn't come in this way. He came by ambulance. He came bleeding down Main Street a hundred miles an hour with a bullet in his head.

Instant. What's more instant than a bullet to the head? And yet he's here. And not here. I don't know what they mean by *dissociative*. If I were to go up there, would he know who I am? Does he know who he is? If he could do what he did, then Ben didn't want to be Ben. He wanted out of his life and mine.

I stare off into traffic. "I just want to say again, if you feel like you need to do this out of some sense of obligation or—or restitution or whatever—you don't."

Francis watches people pass on the sidewalk. "I'm a priest, Maggie." He flicks his collar. "I realize that scenes like last night make it a little hard to believe, but I am. And that means showing up. Even if all I'm able to do is listen."

On the other side of the road, a homeless man stands on the corner with a harmonica in one hand and an empty milk carton in the other. He breathes in and out on the mouthpiece and sends a tuneless whinny into the air as he shakes the milk carton at passersby. A young black woman in a fitted suit slows as she passes him. She pulls a bill from the side pocket of her purse and drops it into the carton. As she continues down the sidewalk, he shouts, "God bless you, beautiful!" and wolf-whistles into his harmonica. The woman hikes her purse up her shoulder and keeps moving.

"Ben has this thing," I say, "where he can't pass a street person without giving them money." I crack the window for some air. "Even if he's totally broke. Even if all he can manage is a couple of quarters. I really got on him about it once, you know—'Hey, we're broke and here you are giving this guy money to buy booze.' I told him he should volunteer at a shelter if he was so fired up about it. The next time we walked by some homeless lady, he kept going. To shut me up, I suppose. We got home and he . . . he just couldn't take it. He turned around and drove back downtown. We drove round and round looking for this woman."

"Doesn't sound like such a bad impulse," Francis says.

"But he didn't want to admit why we were driving back. He—"

Knuckles rap the passenger window and we both start.

"Father Luke!" A silver-haired woman smiles in at us, waving.

"Mrs. Mundy! Hello!" Francis rolls his window down. "How nice to see you!"

"Oh, Father Luke! It's you." Mrs. Mundy must be one of his parishioners. She looks so pleased to see him that maybe she hasn't seen DRUNK PRIEST PROPOSITIONS COPS.

She leans down a little more and looks in at me. "Hello,"

she says with a slightly curt nod. Maybe she *has* seen the news.

"Mrs. Mundy, this is my sister, Maggie."

"Oh!" she says. "Nice to meet you. We're all so very fond of your brother, Maggie. So fond." Tears come to her eyes and she puts a small clawlike hand to her temple as if she needs a moment to get her words back. "I can't tell you how happy I am to see you, Father Luke. Everyone's been asking when you'll be back."

Francis takes a big nervous breath and then says, "That's kind of you. Thank you. I, ah, well, I'm going to be away for a little while. I'm going on a, ah, a retreat."

Her face turns serious. She grips my brother's arm with one hand and leans on the car door with the other. "You do what you need to do, but you just know that we love you. You're our priest." She looks across to me and says, "Father Luke made our church into a place we want to be. And it doesn't matter what they say—we don't care about any of that. It won't be our place without him in it."

Francis lays his hand over hers. "Thank you. You have no idea how much that means to me."

"No need for thanks, it's the truth. What you did for Fiona Reagan, what you did for Edward Kelly and his family. And you and I both know—we all know—that Donald Kane wouldn't be alive if it weren't for you. We are not a church without you. You're our priest."

My brother picks up her hand and kisses it. And the sight of his kiss knots in my throat along with *You think I don't have pain?* And *Why the priesthood?*

"When you're ready, we're ready," Mrs. Mundy says and

presses her own lips to the spot on her hand where Father Luke kissed her. She gives him a stiff little nod, and pats his arm a last time. "God bless you. We'll see you soon."

I wipe my eyes and watch her scurry down the street, pulling her nylon windbreaker closed against the wind.

Francis presses his fingertips to his forehead.

I can't manage to swallow and I can't find the right words either. "That was really nice," I say at last.

Dropping his hands into his lap, Francis straightens his back and takes another fortifying breath. "I'm heading up. I'll give you a call later."

"Do you want me to wait at the coffeehouse on the corner? I don't have to meet Lucy until—"

"I'll call you." He takes my hand and kisses the back of it just like he did with Mrs. Mundy.

A sudden wave of loneliness washes over me—loneliness and gratitude—as he picks up his shoulder bag. He touches his collar once more and gets out of the car.

TEN

Ben

Today's lunch sits by the bed. Gray is melting off the mashed potatoes, threatening the white, white room. Dr. Lambert's already been and gone.

Sonuvabitch started in again with "Why don't you want to be Ben? What is the most frightening thing about being Ben?"

Who the hell *would* want to be Ben?

Ben made his own skin crawl, and it's never coming back.

From the doorway of the white, white room, the view of the ward is a charming shade of Technicolor gloom. Nurses trot by in their rubber clogs, and daisy-covered scrubs, scrubs with teddy bears and scrubs with polka dots, as if they all made a wrong turn on the way to the kids' ward. A couple of patients shuffle from their rooms, carrying their lunch trays down the hall to the common room so they can watch TV.

"Ben? You're Ben, right?"

Ah look, if it isn't Greg, the Attorney. Doesn't he clean up pretty. All ready to head back downtown and lawyer someone out of his life savings.

"I'm sure I deserve that," Greg says. "I just wanted to apologize. I went off my meds."

Greg the Attorney sounds almost bashful today.

He keeps going. "I said a lot of crazy shit during our group session, some threatening words that were inexcusable."

Greg shifts his smile down the hall and then back. He looks at the name card slotted beside the door to the white, white room.

Can't believe everything you read, Greg.

"I'm being discharged today and I wanted you to know that I wish you peace, man."

If you want peace, prepare for war.

Off goes Greg the Attorney. He's got a butter-soft calf-skin carry bag with him. He pauses at the nurses' station. He speaks, they giggle. Imagine if Cola had been born with a silver spoon up his ass. A grinning orderly arrives with a wheelchair.

"Ah," says Greg. "I see you've brought my Porsche around." He sits and the orderly takes hold of the chair's push handles, turning Greg toward the exit. The buzzer sounds and the unit doors open wide and say, *Awe,* because who isn't in awe of Greg the Attorney?

Between here and Greg's chariot, a woman steps into the hall with her lunch tray. The black jeans still sag around her hips and her gray sweater continues to drip off her bones. Gwen. She turns to watch Greg being turned loose on an unsuspecting world. Sic 'em, Greg.

Gwen heads this way, her starved deer legs overshadowed

by her starved deer eyes that roam to and fro as if she's keeping an eye out for wolves. EverythingsGoneSinceMySonDied Gwen.

She creeps along, looking past her lunch tray, picking her way across the rough terrain. When she catches her reflection in a smoked glass door, she ducks her chin and averts her eyes.

She pauses at the entrance to the common room, getting her bold up. It ain't easy but she'd rather be alone in a crowd than alone in her own white, white room.

If Ben were in his skin, he might go after Gwen to see what happens next. Ben may not be here, but his skin can still crawl.

Gwen has made it to the middle of the common room. She looks from the kitchenette in one corner to the television in the other. The television is bolted to both the wall and a *Murder, She Wrote* marathon. Angela Lansbury's face is oh-so-soothing to the St. Anthony psych ward: porridge made flesh.

Gwen turns from the screen. She pauses to look at a painting on the wall, framed under Plexiglas. She ducks her chin again. Must have caught another glimpse of her reflection. Gwen wants no part of Gwen.

If Ben were standing at the entrance to the common room, he'd home in on Gwen right away. He'd recollect the day he walked into the bathroom and the mirror was gone. And then the mirror in the bedroom disappeared and the mirror in the hall. When all reflections disappear, it's only a matter of time until the ghost goes with them. Gwen might not know this.

She finally chooses the table in the darkest corner.

Perhaps Gwen would like to dine with the skinbag formerly known as Ben.

It's Gwen, right? Mind sharing a table?

Disappearing Gwen faces her tray and says, "That's fine." She doesn't make eye contact. Maybe she is afraid she'll see her reflection there too.

How to explain: There is no here, here.

There are now two lunch trays on Gwen's table, each one daring the faithful: take, eat. This is the gruel, which is given for you.

Gwen unwraps her plastic fork, blinks at her own tray and then at the duplicate one across from her.

These green beans look like they washed up on the rocks somewhere.

Her tight mouth crooks and she says, "Yes. That is what they look like."

Her eyes flick to the ceiling and then off to the side. She looks over to a table with a young woman in pajamas. Seated opposite pajama-girl is her mirror image dressed in street clothes.

"That's her sister." Gwen keeps her eyes on the women. She adds, "I always thought it would be neat to have a twin. All the people you could fool."

Some people only fool themselves.

Gwen looks at their feet, the slippers on one pair, sneakers on the other. "I always wanted a sister. Or a brother. Someone you could tell things to." She looks back at her plate. "I guess it doesn't always work out the way you hope."

What was his name?

Gwen is quiet a second. Then she says, "Nicolas. We called him Nicky when he was little."

Nicolas? Nicky. Not Cola, Nicky.

How did he die?

"He fell, I mean, he—he jumped. Off a roof." Gwen's face crumples. "Maybe if I could've been there, I could have . . . It could have come out differently. He wouldn't talk to me. He had a drug problem."

Ben had a brother with a drug problem. A problem with a drug brother.

"Ben?" Gwen asks. "Is he your . . . ?"

Ben had a son too. And a wife. And he had a brother to talk to, but that didn't make a difference. They all went out the window.

Gwen looks up. She looks right where Ben's eyes should be.

Ben could have saved them all. But he killed them all instead and they killed him right back. Right back. Shot in the back. Even Cola. Even Ben's baby brother. Cola got the last laugh, didn't he? Of course maybe there's a black hole in Cola's head too, just like this one, but deep enough to hold ten grand.

Gwen looks at the bandage. She squints at it, trying to see if the black hole makes any more sense than the mouth.

"Who is Ben?" She looks toward the door and her face turns tense and soft at once. As if she's seen a lover. Her breath catches.

She watches someone come closer until he stops right here. "Hello, Father," she says.

Black-sleeved arms lead up to a white collar. "Hello. Hi, Ben."

Gwen looks from the priest to the skinbag across from her. "You're Ben?"

Well, well. Look who's come to deliver the last rites. Won't he be sorry. Show's over, folks, nothing to save here.

"It's me, Francis, Maggie's brother," the priest says and extends his hand.

No kidding. This is the bughouse, Father, not the Federation for the Blind.

Francis nods and smiles. "Gee, it looks like I've interrupted your lunch. Perhaps I should come back another time."

"No!" Gwen looks up at Maggie's brother as though he's got her heart wrapped in swaddling clothes. "Won't you join us?"

"I wouldn't want to intrude," he says.

Ben wouldn't want him to either. Gwen's a different story though. Gwen is like Maggie is like Miriam is like, *No intrusion. Please, have a seat.*

Francis sets his bag down and pulls out a chair. He opens a sweating bottle of cold water and takes a slug. "It's a warm one today. They actually sent me to the wrong room—I ended up in Ben Brody Sr.'s room! He was sleeping so I didn't get a chance to say hello. Have you seen him?"

Ben's old man is in this building? No. Yes. Of course he is. Is he still in restraints? Is he still sucking up bags of blood?

"He's doing well," Francis says. "Apparently, he's even going for little rambles around the unit. Should be going home soon."

"Are you a Catholic priest?" Gwen asks.

"I am indeed." Francis opens his bottle of water again. "It's nice that you have a place to eat besides your room."

There's no elbow room in the white, white room.

Not enough room to swing a cat. At least there's murder in here.

A bead of sweat trickles off the good reverend's temple. He looks over his shoulder. "Oh, right. I like Angela Lansbury as much as the next guy, but six in a row?"

Gwen laughs, ingratiating herself to the white collar.

Yes, the common room, where it all happens: group therapy, TV, and a bookshelf brimming with board games. A lunatic's wet dream.

Gwen has no ears for the skinbag anymore. It's all about the collar. It's all about God's mouthpiece strumming her pain with his fingers.

"Father?" Gwen scans the face of Francis. "Could you, um—my son died."

Her eyes fill and flood and the waves roll down her cheeks. She touches his sleeve.

Francis covers her hand with his big soft palm. "Can you tell me your name?"

She tells him.

Oh, Gwen, come off it. There is nothing holy about the Father or the Son and you don't want to get anywhere near that Spirit. Ask Ben, he knows. Ben's had his ass kicked from one end of hell to the other.

"I haven't been to church since I was a little girl," she says. "I don't think I know how to pray anymore . . . Maybe you could say, um, say a blessing. For Nicolas. And me."

Go ahead, Padre, kill her softly with your song.

"I imagine everyone has felt at one time or another like he doesn't know how to ask for help," Francis tells her. "There's a beautiful verse in Romans that says, 'For we do not know how to pray as we ought, but the Spirit intercedes for us with sighs too deep for words.'"

Gwen slides her other hand under the big palm of Francis and he begins his blessing. "The old order has passed away: Lord, please welcome Nicolas into paradise, where there is no sorrow . . ."

Even through a desert storm, Ben can hear prayers for the dead.

" . . . no weeping or pain but the fullness of peace and joy with your Son and the Holy Spirit forever and ever. Please deliver your servant Gwen from every sorrow and let her find your peace, which is beyond all understanding." Francis brings his hand to Gwen's forehead and makes the sign of the cross with his thumb.

Like a fugitive from mercy, Ben ducks and squints, trying to see past all those mothers milling in the tunnel of his vision: Gwen and Maggie and Miriam, all the mothers of all the sons shivering in the outlands.

TEN

Maggie

It's twenty past three when I park Lucy's car out front of her building. Today is her eighty-first birthday. Feels like about eighty-one years since I sat there in that bus shelter watching bulldozers and dump trucks across the road. It's quiet over there now. Looks like they finished digging and have poured a foundation. There is something naked and pitiable about the sight of those concrete slabs and fresh gray walls.

No word yet from Francis. There are no missed calls on my cell phone. No messages. What could he be doing over there at St. Anthony?

Can't bring myself to call. I'm almost afraid he would put Ben on the phone. Or maybe I'm afraid that he wouldn't be able to put Ben on the phone.

I should be there, I should be there, I should be there, calling out to Ben until he answers me. I should be reaching into the quicksand and dragging Ben out, wiping away the muck and the mire until he sees us again.

Before it all went to shit, Ben and I could always find a way through. We could kick our way out of the black box, make it into something else, something powerless against us. Maybe we just forgot how.

When Frankie was fourteen weeks, he got a fever. No infection, the doctor said. He's just caught your cold, she said. His temperature should be down by tomorrow. I blew my nose and quietly despised her for not fixing him immediately. What was she getting paid for if not omnipotence?

Back at the apartment, Frankie wailed. He wouldn't stop. I held him tight and paced. "I'm sorry," I told him. "I'm so sorry." I blew my nose and looked at Ben. "I shouldn't even be holding him. Goddamn Typhoid Mary over here."

Ben held me by the shoulders and sat us at the dining table. He took my snotty tissue and threw it in the garbage. "Look at me," he said. "It's not your fault. It's a cold. He's going to be fine. Why don't I make you some ginger tea and then you feed him and it'll be like you're both—"

"We have to call Francis," I blurted, Frankie's overheated head against my chin.

Ben stared at me.

"Right now. Please."

He didn't argue. He dialed and handed me the phone.

"Frankie's sick," I said into the receiver. "His fever won't come down. I'm scared." I didn't need to tell Francis what I wanted.

"It's okay, honey," he said. "Sit tight. I'll be there in half an hour."

No smart-ass remarks. God knows I would have deserved them. I'd been so smug when I told my brother that Ben and

I had gotten married at the courthouse. We don't need a bunch of hocus pocus to make our lives work, I said, so don't expect a baptism either.

Francis doesn't hold a grudge. He was there in exactly thirty minutes. He wore his clerical shirt.

I kissed his cheek. "Thank you for coming so quick."

"You're not kidding. I didn't even have time to put my face on." Francis winked and took my hand.

I choked out a little laughter as my eyes welled up—the sight of him, the feel of his big gentle hand. I followed my brother through the living room to the little dining table off the kitchen. I let his hand go and watched him open his knapsack, take out his prayer book and the holy water and anointing oil. He set candles on the table and lit them.

Ben came out of the bedroom with the baby. Frankie was quieter now. Ben glanced at the flickering table and gave me a look of bewilderment.

I looked back at him, willing him: *Just let me have this. I need this magic right now. I need it.*

"Hi Ben," Francis said. "Sounds like you guys are having a tough day." He laid his hand on the crown of his nephew's head. "Hey Frankie-boy, how're you feeling?" Frankie blinked up, his mouth crooked and burbling. "Ah, you're okay. He looks good." Francis glanced from me to Ben. "You had me worried there."

Ben nodded and the two of them exchanged a look.

"Okay," I interrupted. "Are we ready?"

Francis smiled at Frankie. "You ready, handsome?"

My brother's voice was low and gentle as he began. "Some people define baptism as a washing away of sin, but there is another tradition that sees it as the watering of seed, nurturing the soul for new life . . ."

The flickering candles, Frankie's quiet babble, and the scent of the oil as Francis made the sign of the cross on Frankie's forehead . . . it was all so dreamlike that I calmed and steadied.

The next morning, Frankie's temperature was back to normal. He lay on the bed between Ben and me.

Propped up on one elbow, Ben took a sip of coffee, swallowed, and smirked at me. "*I will never—*" he paused for effect. "—*ever baptize my kid. And that is that.*"

That was me he was quoting, a six months' pregnant me.

I kept my eyes on Frankie. "Could you give your daddy a message?"

Frankie wrapped his fingers around my thumb.

Ben went on. "*We may as well wave a dead chicken at our baby.*"

"Tell him," I said to Frankie, "that he's a big-mouth jerk-weasel."

Ben coughed and spit coffee on himself.

Frankie hiccupped into laughter. Ben glanced at me, and the three of us giggled like maniacs.

Twisting my wedding band now, I try to hold on to that echo of our old selves, but as I look at the new foundation across the road an old Sunday morning warning comes to mind, the one about the foolish man who built his house on sand: *The rain fell, the floods came, and the winds blew and beat against that house, and it fell with a mighty crash.*

Could anyone have withstood this kind of wind and rain? How can you hold or be held in a storm like that?

I used to think that between the two of us, we could weather it all. When Ben met my gaze, he looked so certain of us that I was sure he could hold me to the earth, keep me from blowing away. And then I walked out. I'm the one who left. Now, when I hear the click of that door closing behind me, it's like a gunshot.

What if there is no Ben left anymore? Just like that: click.

My ring feels loose. In the passenger seat is a clear plastic box. The chocolate cake inside is iced with *Happy Birthday, Lucy!* I check my watch. Last night, after Francis walked out, I lay in bed thinking of all the closing doors, all the clicks I'd ever heard. Sometime after midnight I remembered that Lucy was officially eighty-one years old. All she wants is to find a way back through that closed door, to find Lloyd. I turned on the light, grabbed my laptop, and looked up Monique Fontaine, professional medium. "She's the best," Lucy had said.

Monique's web site said that she was humbled and honored to be an Ambassador for the Spirit World.

I sent an email to Monique. In the morning, I phoned and the medium picked up. She had heard from Lucy a couple of days earlier, she said.

"I felt very bad that I could not be with her on her birthday and then last night, I had a cancellation! I was going to come to the Tea and Spirit Gathering and make a nice surprise for her." Monique Fontaine's accent matched her name. French, I think, but I'm bad with accents.

I asked Monique if she'd be willing to make a house call. A private sitting. "I could pay you," I said.

"Ah! Such a beautiful idea! When I talked to Lucy the

other day she said so many good-good things about you and
she is right!"

In my side mirror now, a bus roars up the road and pauses
at the curb to let off passengers. As soon as the bus moves
out, I notice an old white Toyota putter up behind and cruise
along until the driver discovers a parking spot a couple of
cars ahead of me.

A short squat woman gets out. That must be the Ambassador now. The picture on Fontaine's web site was a little
younger, a little thinner. I pick up the cake box and get out
too, just in case. Hustling to the sidewalk I stand in front of
Lucy's building.

The woman ambles toward me. "Ah! You must be Maggie!"

"Yes!" A part of me is startled. Then I remember the cake
in my hands: *Happy Birthday, Lucy!* "Monique?"

We shake hands. Glancing at the puffy black bow tied at
the neck of her peach blouse, the gold St. Christopher medal
dangling, I feel an odd pleasure at how ordinary she looks—
like somebody's auntie, like the receptionist who worked for
our family dentist when Francis and I were kids. The lack of
drama lends Monique Fontaine a potential authenticity in
my eyes.

"Lucy will be happy to see you," I tell her. A strange little
tingle of excitement comes into my belly. Almost the way I
felt the first time I decorated the apartment for Ben's birthday. I got up in the morning and blew up balloons for him,
dangled some streamers. He'd been chauffeuring people
around half the night and didn't wake until noon. When he
stumbled into the living room, all bed-head and frog-throat,

he looked at the blues and pinks and yellows on the wall and lit up as though he'd never seen a balloon before.

I glance down again at the chocolate cake and for the first time in ages it feels like I'm doing something right.

The two of us walk to the intercom. I buzz 1414. Monique puts a finger to her lips and winks.

A few moments later, the scratchy speaker comes on and Lucy shouts, "Maggie? Come on up." The lock buzzes.

Monique and I head into the lobby and circumvent the huge dry fountain, its stone cherub holding tight to its open-mouthed fish.

"This fountain kills me," I say. "It must weigh a ton. How did they even get it in here?"

Monique giggles. "Maybe it was the only thing left standing from the old place and they had to build around it!"

When the elevator doors open, I smile at the thought: a dancing baby, oblivious to oblivion.

As soon as the car lifts off, I feel that same flock of black birds erupt in my belly, just as I did the first time I came here. Like recollection and premonition at once. The memory of rushing out through Lucy's front doors, full of tears and rage, feels as though it happened eons ago, as though I have run in a big noisy circle and found myself back where I started, ready to try again. "How long have you known Lucy?"

"Let me see. She came to me the first time, I think, one and a half years ago. I got such a kick out of her."

The doors open and we head down the shag carpet corridor. Monique continues. "She had this terrible loss from her husband and yet she had so much faith and joy."

Outside 1414 we can hear Tammy Wynette singing "Stand by Your Man." Monique hums along and I give the door a good rap so that Lucy will hear over the music.

From inside: "Coming!" Tammy Wynette quiets down and a few seconds later Lucy pulls open the door.

"Happy birthday!"

Lucy squeals. "Monique! Monique is here. How did you— how?"

Monique throws her arms wide. Lucy pushes her walker aside and Monique steps in to give her a hug. "Your very nice friend, Maggie, she called on me. And for your birthday she hires me for a private sitting!"

Lucy releases Monique. "And a cake! For me!" It's as if Lucy's whole body is smiling. I hold the cake in one hand and give her a hug.

"*Mwaaa!*" she says as she plants a pink-lipsticked kiss on my cheek. "Thank you, dear. My day is always brighter when I see you."

It is? I've felt like such a troll, the idea that I might bring about any luminosity is a surprise. "You're very welcome. Happy birthday!"

"Come sit down!" Lucy says. She pushes the door closed. "We'll have our own little Tea and Spirit Gathering right here!" She looks me up and down. "You look cute. I like that shirt, I like how it rhymes with your pants."

"Thanks. You two sit and I'll put the kettle on." I head to the kitchen with the cake. As water fills the kettle, I'm struck with the realization that I'm glad to feel wanted—glad there is some place I'm supposed to be.

"What a treat it is to see you," Lucy tells Monique and then calls out, "Earl Grey for us and whatever you'd like for yourself. Teapot's in the cupboard beside the fridge. Tea is beside the stove."

Kettle on, I pull a pack of candles from my pocket and start poking a circle of eight into the cake and then one in the middle as I listen to them chatter in the next room.

"You know, Lucy, it is also my grandson's birthday this week. He will be five years old and I would like to buy for him *Pennywhistle Pig*," she says and laughs. Her speech is peppered with sudden bursts of laughter. "And maybe you could sign the book for him."

"Of course!" Lucy is getting bubblier by the moment. She instructs Monique on where to find a new copy on her bookshelf.

"I love this pig!" Another burst of giggles from Monique. "Let me pay you for this now before I forget."

"No! It's a gift. What's your grandson's name?"

"His name is Pascal." She begins to spell it for Lucy.

"Sorry about my handwriting. My eyes . . ."

"No, no, it's wonderful. My grandson, he is going to go crazy for this pig. Lucy, you are a real writer the way you make this pig come alive! Oh my God—when he dances with his little trotters and the flute!" She erupts with more laughter. Lucy joins in.

"Can we ask about that?" Lucy says. "I've been thinking about another Pennywhistle story and maybe the spirit guide will have a message for me."

"Yes, yes, we must find out what we can about the piggy!"

Lucy calls out, "Maggie, Monique is psychic too. You can ask her questions about what's happening in your life and the future!"

A slow boiling whistle comes up from the stove as though the kettle can't quite believe its ears. "Oh yeah?" I call and take the kettle off the burner.

I pour hot water in the pot, then set it on a tray with cups and saucers. Fitting the little cake front and center, I light the candles before I pick up the tray. I begin singing, "Happy birthday to you . . ." as I creep toward the living room.

Monique sings along and Lucy joins in, singing to herself, smiling with glee. I set the tray on the coffee table. Lucy takes a big breath and blows out the nine candles.

Monique and I clap.

"Look at this," Lucy says. "You girls are too much! My first message ever came from Monique. She is the best!"

Monique grins. "Aww, Lucy, you are my sweetheart. I will always remember that night. The love and light in the room was so *strong*. You know how they say, 'Parting is such sweet sorrow'? There is nothing so sweet as a message from Spirit."

I take the teapot from the tray and set cups in front of Lucy and Monique. "Cake now?" I ask. "Or maybe later."

"How about later?" Lucy says. "After our session!"

"Sure." Uncertain what to do next, I ease myself into the armchair and watch the two of them.

"You look suspicious!" Monique says to me. "Don't worry, I'll be gentle."

Lucy and Monique both laugh uproariously at this.

Monique pins me with a maternal, loving expression. "Maggie, I'm just playing, but it's true you do not look so comfortable. I get the sense that you are new to this, so maybe I should start by telling you some things about what I do. I'm not an exorcist—you know, one of those mediums who get rid of curses or bad spells." She and Lucy pause for another chortle. "I don't help tortured souls over to the other side like that movie *Poltergeist*. What I do is help link those who are no longer incarnated on earth with the loved ones who are still here." She gives me another look of loving serenity and then says, "You still look concerned, Maggie. What are you worried about?"

"Oh no, nothing. I'm just . . . taking it all in." I'm not worried exactly. That tingle of excitement keeps coming into my belly, that feeling of anticipation, as if something is going to happen at any moment. I don't know what it means. Or what I want it to mean.

Lucy leans over and fills the cup in front of Monique and then her own.

"The spirits I communicate with most are your loved ones, friends, spirit guides, and sometimes pets who are in spirit. These are the spirits who watch over you while you're here on the earth. I'm like a telephone line. I deliver messages. If you have someone in mind, don't tell me who it is. When I feel a presence, I'll ask you for some type of confirmation of who is coming through and the reason I do this is to get a clear sense of the spirit's relationship to you and also to give you proof of the afterlife. You can ask me questions as we go. Okay?"

Lucy reaches toward me with a cup of milky tea. I take it from her, little electric shocks still zipping through my guts.

Monique takes up her cup and sips before she releases a long, happy sigh. Lucy does the same as though it's part of a ritual they share. She reaches for the basket at the base of her walker and yanks a couple of tissues from the box.

Monique sets her cup down. "Okay. Why don't we begin to center ourselves? Are we ready?"

I lay my hands on my anxious stomach.

"We're going to take some breaths," she says. "As you exhale I want you to have the intent of detaching from this physical world so that we can move into a sacred space." Monique takes a deep breath through her nose and exhales with an *ahhh*. She closes her eyes. "Yes, detach, detach . . ." She and Lucy continue to breathe slowly and audibly.

I watch them a moment and then give in, close my eyes, and take my own slow, deep breaths.

"Detach from the stress of demands and schedules. Leave all that behind so we can make a beautiful sacred space. Breathe in . . . detach, detach, that's it, just do that nice sigh as you exhale . . . and now I'll say a prayer. *Infinite Spirit, Divine Father-Mother-God, we ask for a blessing on this sitting. We ask for the highest and the best, clarity of mind, direction and understanding. Amen.*"

Monique opens her eyes and lets loose with another playful laugh. "Maggie, when I start this giggle, it is just spirit talking. It's a lovely feeling actually, and it makes me feel sparkling all over. As I was saying the prayer, and we all moved into that sacred space, there was this beautiful influx of energy that came in and I felt angels with that. Do you understand, please? Do you believe in angels?" She looks at me but doesn't wait for an answer. "I feel Lucy's, but I also feel yours. You have these beautiful angelic beings around you who have been supporting you and holding you through the challenges in this life and as they come forward—I have three of them and they say that due to your personality—which can be pretty steadfast, I hear, stubborn . . ."

"Oh yes," says Lucy as though she knows me all too well.

Monique giggles, but remains in her vaguely trancelike state. "And as you evolved there was an open mind that occurred, but still, it's an attitude of '*Show me the evidence so that I can believe.*' And I have a lady that is coming forward—Yes, thank you—and I hear Mother. Do you have a grandmother who is in spirit, please?"

I don't want to sit here being a cranky skeptic, but it's hard not to roll my eyes at that one. What is the likelihood that anyone of us here has a living grandmother?

"She feels very motherly, this lady, full of vim and vigor—Yes, thank you—and I feel that this lady would have had a lineage that took her to back to Europe. And she is pointing to Lucy. Lucy, do you have a grandmother of European ancestry—Yes, thank you—or Irish or Scottish, please?"

It finally occurs to me that her asides of "Yes, thank you," are acknowledgments to some unseen entity's extra tip.

"Yes!" Lucy is bursting with anticipation.

"Did you know this grandmother, please?"

"I met her."

"You met her. Well, this grandmother, she comes in with a very strong nature but a very loving nature. Do you understand, please?"

Lucy frowns. "She and my mother didn't get along. My mother was afraid of her."

"Yes, she is a strong presence and a stubborn presence. She claims that you are very much like her. Do you understand, please?"

"Well, Lloyd always said I was a stubborn girl! That's why I can relate to Maggie. She could be my daughter!"

"She's telling me that you have this strong idea of what is right and wrong. And this is a virtue that you endeavor to live by. And she is saying that she has regrets about her life. But she is with her daughter in spirit—your mother—and they have come to understand one another. They have reconciled their differences and the love is there. She is saying that she hopes you will focus your stubborn nature into goodness, into your art—Yes, thank you—She's holding up three books. Oh Lucy! And a little pig, there is a tiny little pig in her palm. She says you are going to create three more books for children—because the core of you is all about saving the children. Particularly sensitive children who have the ability to see, to ah, ah—Yes, thank you—to be aware of higher frequencies and you want to gather the children who have been misunderstood because you have been misunderstood throughout your life."

"Yes!" Lucy says. "Even when I was a little girl. I was a very sensitive child."

"Yes, but she says that in your seventies, life changed for you. You had an awakening to your creativity. I feel that, for you, the years from seventy-five to eighty-five are all about breaking through the final veils and making a name for yourself. She says you're going to channel your energy to help the parents of children who are highly sensitive. Oh I'm *really* excited about this, Lucy! I feel your life changed at the age of seventy-nine. You entered into a whole new frequency. Your physical body is having a hard time keeping up with the frequencies of your spirit, but you are catching up. Your author spirit guide—I get the name James—James is saying that when you give yourself time to meditate, he will come to give you the visions. You're very intuitive, Lucy. It's not by chance that you write and I feel that you are going to invest in a world-changing endeavor. I'd say from eighty-one to about ninety-one is for doing that. Do you understand, please?"

"Yes!" Lucy looks at me, rapturous and vindicated. "This is just what I wanted to talk about: Pennywhistle Pig and children. And here you've answered me. Thank you, James!"

"Yes, thank you," Monique says. "James says that music is very important to you. You should play music as you write these new books." Monique suddenly sits up. "Did you ever have a miscarriage, please, Lucy? A stillborn child? I have a child with me, a very young child. A boy."

Lucy shakes her head and gives a solemn nod in my direction.

"Oh yes, yes," Monique says. "He is pointing to you, Maggie. Not stillborn. He is holding up two fingers. He's telling me that he is two years old." Monique nods and giggles. "So cute. He's—Yes, thank you—he's making a frowny face and he's doing this"—Monique turns her palm to the ceiling and pumps it up—"like he's saying more. He's more than two, but not quite three. Do you understand, please?"

My stomach detonates with shooting stars. I'm afraid to move.

"He's holding out his arms to you. He's laughing. He's very happy. Did you know a little boy who would be in spirit?" Monique giggles and it's cut short with a gasp. "Oh!" She puts a hand to her head. "Some kind of head injury. He hit his head. This is how he died." Monique puts both hands on her skull as though she's trying to hold it in one piece.

Oh God. Oh Frankie. Please be here. Please tell me you're here.

"Take it away, please, take it away," Monique says and then eases her hands from her head. "Yes, thank you—I feel so much love from him. I'm hearing 'Mother.' Do you have a child in spirit, Maggie? Do you understand this, please?"

Heat and sparks race up and down my limbs. My Frankie. You've found me.

Face in my hands, I nod and whisper, "Yes."

"He is all love and he is so filled with joy. He says that you gave him joy. You made him laugh. He's showing me peanut butter. Do you understand, please?"

The sparks ease and a tender wash of love comes over me, up my legs, into my belly and I feel him. It's Frankie. It's you, baby. This is what I want. This is all I want. He's in my lap again, the weight of him. The weight of his memory, me and Ben and Frankie. He's almost two. A jar of peanut butter on the table, a bag of bread. Frankie dips my finger into the jar and then puts it into his own mouth. He doesn't want it on bread, doesn't want it off the spoon; he wants it off my finger. "What are you doing, weirdo?" Ben laughing. Like Frankie, but deeper. "You are such a little weirdo," Ben says. My Ben. The real Ben, the Ben I can see, the one who can see me. "You're my favorite weirdo in the world," he says. "You and your weirdo mother." Frankie giggles and giggles and pushes my hand into the jar again, takes it out and sticks my finger into Ben's mouth, brown paste smearing down his chin. Giggles and giggles. We are savages. We are goons and we are in love.

Tears stream now, washing down my face.

"He says that sometimes he comes in dreams and he likes

to be in your lap. He thinks you can feel him. He says, 'Don't be afraid.' It's just him watching over you. He wants you to know that he chose you, that he knew he wouldn't be here on this earth a long time, but he chose you and he learned to love through you. He is proud that you are his mother. He says that you are a mother to many, that people turn to you for help and that you are very kind, but that you also need to be kind to yourself. He says that you need a mother too—Yes, thank you—Is your mother in spirit, please?"

The smell of Frankie's fine hair, the way his small perfect head knocks against my clavicle, bone on bone, I feel him.

Melting into the chair. I'm not here, I'm slipping through, into the blue, into forever. Please take me with you. Please, Frankie.

He feels like beauty. He feels like everyone I ever lost, all the need and the want and the failing in my lap. Just to put my arms around him, but I can't move, can't speak.

"I think so," Lucy whispers.

"He says that he is glad you have Lucy in your life. You can mother each other. Do you understand, please? He—ha-ha—he is so cute. So happy and he says—again, he's hold-ing up the jar of peanut butter. In two hands! He's pointing to Lucy and saying that you and Lucy should have peanut butter together, like a mom and kid, and he would be here with you. Don't be sad, he says, because he's always here with you. Always present. He is watching over you. He says that you should never feel sad or guilty because there was nothing you could have done. He chose to come to you and he chose to move into spirit—Yes, thank you—He has a friend, a big yellow dog and—ha-ha—he's introducing you to the dog. I'm hearing the name, Luna. It's like a yellow Lab and there's a man—this man is a fatherly type. I am hearing Father. Is the child's father in spirit, please?"

Drifting, swimming with my laughing boy, we're underwater, under dreams, under the covers, and I can hear the words at the surface but I can't make a sound. Don't break the spell—please, don't leave. Take me with you.

"Yes," murmurs Lucy. "His father's in spirit. Suicide."

"He's come from deep sadness. Did he die after the child, please? Yes, the child says he was there to greet his daddy, to show him the way. Yes. So much pain, he's saying—Yes, thank you—ha-ha—but this man, he's got a great sense of humor. He's playing with the boy. He's happy now. I love his energy and his humor. The name, does it start with an *N*? Or an *M*, a *B*?"

Trying to say no. Like a dream, I don't know if the sound is coming. No. I can't breathe. Stop it. I'm sorry, Frankie. I'm sorry, baby. I love you. Your daddy loves you. He's lost, that's all. Help me find him.

"I'm getting a short name. Is it Tim or Matt? Or . . ."

"No!"

Lucy jumps. Monique blinks at the room as if she's coming out of a stupor.

"Ben is not dead. He is not!" Out of the chair, fingers raking my scalp, my heart booms and sparks. "My husband is—he's alive. My brother is with him right now. He is. He was."

"I thought you—" Lucy's hand covers her mouth; her eyes blink and tear up. "I thought you said—"

"You fed this woman information about me?" I look from Lucy to Monique.

"I am truly sorry," Monique says. "All I could hear was 'father.' I did not know whose father. Is your father in spirit?"

"Please, shut up. No disrespect. Or—maybe yes, disrespect. I feel disrespect. I didn't ask for this. This was for—"

Lucy folds her hands in her lap and swallows. "Maggie, I think there's been a misunderstanding. I did not feed—"

"No more." Palm up, like a stop sign, I go to the kitchen and find my purse. "I think you two should just—"

Behind me, Monique says, "No, no. I'll go."

"No! Please don't go. Either of you," Lucy pleads. "This is my fault. I get overexcited. I should have let you speak for yourself."

When I come back into the living room, Monique and Lucy are on their feet. Monique's face is gentle, and she says to Lucy, "It's absolutely my fault. I don't normally do individual readings with two people. In such a small room the energies are too strong and lines get crossed. It's your birthday and I should have known better."

I'm out of breath. I want Ben. I want to fall into Ben and sob and cry and heave and scream and rock him back to life. Where have we been? In tar, we've been wading through tar.

"Please don't go. We'll do our sessions one at a time. I'll wait in the bedroom," Lucy says. Tears slide down her cheeks. She holds fast to Monique, crumpled like a little girl. "Please?"

"Lucy . . ." Monique says in a soothing voice. "Don't be upset."

"It's Lucy's birthday," I say. "She wants to hear from Lloyd." I pull my purse over my shoulder, open the front door, and then listen to it click behind me.

ELEVEN

Ben

Poor Gwen, she got so filled up on pie in the sky, she had no room for lunch. Deliver your servant Gwen from every sorrow, the man said. Now she's gone back to her room to sleep it off. Sleep away the sorrow and pretend that God gives a flying fuck.

Francis rests his hands on the table, sets his priestly eyes on the husk formerly known as Ben, and says, "I know that Maggie is hurting. I can only imagine how much you must be."

What you don't know won't hurt you. Until it does.

"Has your brother been in to see you?"

Cola, Cola, where is Cola? Running scared. Running his mouth. Kid runs around like a blue-arsed fly, the old man used to say.

"Does he know you're here? Maggie hasn't heard from him. She wondered if he might be in trouble."

Trouble shared is trouble doubled.

"If you want to talk about anything . . . Ben, I'm here as

your friend. But I'm also a priest." Maggie's brother lowers his voice. "Whatever you say, I hold in confidence."

Confidence? Is that code for confession? You want a confession, Father WhatsItLike? You're going to hold it all in confidence? So you can hold all the cards? Don't hold your breath. Confession is good for the hole. Let the black hole confess: If Ben took a bullet, gave a bullet, bit the bullet, he got his, didn't he?

What are you squinting at? What, are you deaf?

Maggie's brother keeps on looking and waiting. "Do you want to talk? Talk to me, Ben. What are you thinking?"

Talk talk talk, fuck you! Did you hear that, Father? Talk is shit. This is shit.

"Okay. Okay." Father's hands come up, his calming palms, and he says, "I hear you, brother. Loud and clear."

Loud and clear, too loud for here.

Lookit, Father, the room's clearing out. It's one thing to be in the madhouse but nobody likes a mad man, do they?

"It's okay," Francis calls to somebody, nobody. "We're fine," he says. "We're just talking."

Who's that? Who're you talking to? Orderlies coming? Hospital bouncers. Bring 'em on! Cuz we're not fine. Nobody's fine.

"Listen to me, Ben—"

No Ben! Not Ben. There is no Ben!

"You're running. You think I don't know about running? Come on, Ben. You know who you are. Stop running. Stand still long enough to take a breath—long enough to ask for help."

Help! Where? Our Father? Father—What a farce. No such

thing. The old man in the sky, the old man in the living room. Sons of bitches can make it all disappear, can't they? Here's a confession for you: Fuck the father. Ben's old man is dead. Should be dead. Wish he was dead. If Ben had balls, he'd have pulled the plug and let the blood spray. Is he dead yet? Can't be, no angels singing.

Fuck the father.

Now we're talking. How's that? More where that came from. Come on, Padre, you want the hole world in your hand?

Fuck the brother too. Baby brother, Cola: That sonuv-abitch was into a loan shark for ten grand. Shoulda told him where to find the little prick. But no, Ben told Cola to call the cops. Cop a plea. Not Cola, he's going to cop it sweet, he figures. He'll figure it out.

He was hiding with his honey bear. Until he burned the lair. So much for honor among thieves. Cola, the fly, he doesn't need you till he needs you.

Now you see him, now you don't. He had a plan all right. The best-laid plan. Got a fucked-up plan to share? Call Ben.

He called Ben to meet him at the old diner off the highway. Cola and his diners.

Ben pulls up in a pink superstretch. "What the hell's going on?"

Cola can't take his eyes off the limo. Jittery, laughing like a tommy gun. "Ha-ha. Pepto-Bismol on wheels. Ha-ha. Bar-bie's Dream Car."

No ride of his own, of course. Just Vera's.

"They trashed my place," he says. "My pillows, my mattress was all hacked open with a butcher knife. Knife was stuck in the floor!" Cola's freaked, scared shitless. He opens the trunk of Vera's car: two big boxes. The shipping bills say, "Creature Care Veterinary."

It's all coming together now. *Vera's a big deal down there. Vera's in charge of ordering for all four clinics.*

Cola pulls out a vial of powder that says Telazol. "It's a painkiller," he says. "And a sedative. It's sweet. You talk to God with this shit. You dream and wake up feeling like truth. Me and Vera did a couple caps of it each. We fell asleep and I woke up first. That's when it hit me. Who needs OxyContin?"

His phone goes off. It's Vera.

"She is pissed, man." Cola checks his voice mail and holds the phone to Ben's ear.

Screaming blue murder. "You stole my fucking keys? You stole my fucking car?" Vera is being investigated. They don't believe her keys were stolen. Vera is going to cut off Cola's balls with a rusty knife.

"Why's she have to make it sound all shitty," he says. "I gotta get her car back. Can you keep the boxes for me?"

"No."

Cola grabs Ben's arm. "There's twenty grand here, easy. I'll split it with you."

"Put it in your closet."

"I can't go home." Cola's tearing up. His hair is flopping in his face. "What if those dudes are there? What if cops are watching? Ben. Please. You're my brother."

ELEVEN

Maggie

Sonuvabitch! What am I *doing*? I've got Lucy's car again. I went tearing out of there, got into her car, and took off. I should have stuck her keys back in her hand and said, "That's it, lady. I'm done."

I'm halfway home now. Tomorrow. First thing in the morning, I'll go back there and nip this whole thing in the bud. I don't think I'm up to the task, I'll tell her. Not right for the job. Maybe I need to work in a basement where there's no interaction with people.

At every red light, I check and recheck my cell phone. Nothing. Nothing from Francis. Nothing from anybody.

Four blocks from the apartment. I can't face my place right now. Don't want to look at those walls. There's nothing in the fridge, but I can't bear a restaurant, making nice-face at someone who's also struggling to make nice-face. Can't be with people and I can't be alone.

Did Francis call yet? Nope. Nothing. The ringer is on. It's definitely on.

Supermarket. That's what I should do. Go and buy a few groceries. Francis and I could cook tonight, while he tells me what happened. How Ben is. Who Ben is.

My brother's black clerical shirt shimmers across my brain. His dog collar. Is he going to tell me that he can't tell me anything? Seal of the Confessional? Priest-penitent privilege?

He has to tell me. He *has* to! He's not going to pick them over me again, is he? He would too. He'd tell me nothing and say he took a vow. Fucker.

Shoving through the front door of Myer's Market, I find his cell number on my phone, and then change my mind.

It's not up to Francis to do your bidding, Maggie. It's up to you to cowboy up and go talk to Ben for yourself. Fuck, fuck, fuck. Fuck me!

Yanking a shopping cart out from the tangled row, I start down the dairy aisle, agitated and full of craving. Goddamn Francis. Goddamn Ben. Goddamn me. Goddamn me all to hell!

I drop a carton of milk into the buggy and keep going. Nose around for cheese, and then toss in a block of cheddar. Basics, just get the basics. I don't want basics. I want a steak. I want to tear into something bloody, and I can't afford it. Why did I go and rent that damn woman a psychic for her birthday? Stupid. Stupid-stupid-stupid!

Shoving the buggy, I jerk to a stop when I see the junk food aisle, wheel it back, and slam into someone else's cart.

"Excuse me." Not a cart, it's a walker. "I'm sorry! I'm—" I just hit some old lady's walker! Christ!

"I'm fine. It's fine." Her head is ducked.

"Cecily?"

The woman sucks air off her lip, tries to turn her walker around, and knocks into a shelf of beans. Cans drop. A little cry escapes. She sputters and gasps as though she is about to hyperventilate. She puts both hands up against her face, holds them there like a child who wants to disappear.

I kneel to pick up two rolling cans of navy beans and put them back on the shelf. "Cecily, it's me, Maggie."

She nods but her hands stay where they are, like bars on a cell. No entry. Her head tilts toward the floor and little whimpers slip through her fingers.

Back on my feet, I drape my arm across her back. "Are you hurt? I'm sorry." I hold her walker steady and lock the wheels. "Here, do you want to sit for a second? Sit on your walker, okay?"

She takes one hand from her face and grabs the handle. I keep hold of her arm as she sits.

"It's Maggie, honey. Do you remember me?"

She spreads the hand that remains on her face, trying to cover as much as she can, trying to make one of us go away. Her back shudders.

"I'm sorry," she says through panting tears.

TWELVE

Ben

What do you think, Father? Think Ben told his dumb-shit brother to go fuck himself?

No way. Where we at? Confession number three? Aiding and abetting.

Yeah, sure, there's Ben on the couch, staring at the TV, his closet full of dog dope. He surfs channel to channel and sips a bottle of Bud. Midnight and it's nothing but infomercials. Girls in bikinis: *Call me!* He turns the TV off.

Silence. You gotta know what that's like, Father. Alone with yourself? Quiet crawls into your ears, slithers down your back.

If he could just sleep. Sweet, luscious sleep. He turns the TV back on.

He thinks of Maggie. Fucking Maggie. She walked right out the goddamn door. Until death do us part? Whose death? Ben was still breathing.

Fuck her! He should call her. Tell her what he thinks. He

picks up his cell phone. Don't do it. She doesn't want to talk to you. What's it going to fix? He opens the photo stream: Maggie with Frankie on her lap. Frankie. He never hurt anyone. Look at his little damp hands on her face. Ben stares so long, he can feel hands on his own face.

Then the phone buzzes. Cola.

"Where are you?"

"Listen, don't be pissed with me. I meant to take it with me. I don't even know how to shoot it."

Shoot it? Shoot what? The boxes. What the fuck else is in those boxes? "Cola! You better get this shit out of my place."

"I will. Listen, if you can't sleep, I made some capsules. I'll call you." And he's gone.

Ben looks inside one box and then the other: vials and vials, a bag full of capsules lying on top. And then, wedged down the side, he sees the black butt.

Ever held a gun, Father? It's a revolver, SMITH & WESSON down one side of the barrel, .22 LONG RIFLE down the other. Stainless steel. Shiny as hell. He sits on the edge of the coffee table and cradles it like a baby. He opens the cylinder. Brass bullets in all six chambers.

You think he didn't think about it? Can you go to hell just for thinking about it?

He put it back. Just go to sleep, right? That's all he wanted. He wanted his life back and his son back, but he'd settle for sleep: A long, dreamless sleep, years and years of sleep.

Every time he closes his eyes, he hears Cola. "It's a pain-killer. And a sedative. You talk to God with this shit."

Twenty minutes go by. Thirty.

He goes into the closet, grabs the sandwich bag.

Takes one capsule, lets it roll down his palm.

Yes or no, yes or no?

He sucks it into his mouth and follows with a swig of beer.

Half an hour later, his eyes snap open. Cola said they took a couple each. He opens the bag and takes two more, has another slug of beer.

Then he hears it hunched under the couch, like a toad waiting to be licked. He puts his hand under, feels the old man's vial. Bless me, Father, for I have sinned. Take as needed, the label says. Fuck it. He pops the top, pours in the blue pill. Tastes like mint. He bites into it, grinds it to powder, and waits.

A minute passes, an hour? Then Ben is sleeping in a meadow. Sunlight, warm earth. Sweet. Just like the man said. He turns his head and sees Frankie running in the grass. Squealing, laughing. He climbs onto Ben's chest and takes his face in his hands.

Ben inhales Frankie's peanut butter breath. Kid says, "Don't be pissed-off at me. I don't even know how to shoot it."

Ben's eyes open to the barrel of a Smith & Wesson, Frankie's hands wrapped around the gun. The barrel jiggles when he laughs. "Ha-ha. Barbie's Dream Car."

Ben brings his hands up. Frankie squeezes the trigger and the sky explodes.

His eyes snap open. He's alive. He's on the couch.

A naked man crouches on the coffee table, knees up like a gargoyle. The man smiles.

Guess who. Face-to-face. "If you're me, then who am I?"

The other Ben giggles and shatters in the dark.

Ben sits up. The TV is off, but he can hear kids' music. Xylophones. He feels the weight of another body behind him. Hands on his shoulders, breath in his ear. Words vibrate through his bones: "You're already nobody."

He throws an elbow back, hears the smash. Heart pounding, he looks at the lamp on the floor. The ceramic body is a doll's now, blood leaking from its cracked skull. Eyes lit from within. He kneels and the breath is in his ear again: "Easy, Killer." And the words pull him inside out until he is standing inside his own skull. Clothes melt against his skin. He pulls off his shirt and flesh peels with it. "Get out of my head!"

And just like that, he is sucked back through his own eye sockets, the eyes of the planet, the eyes of God. Falling through the air in a rush of embryonic sludge, he lands with a squelch on his couch.

TWELVE

Maggie

I t's my fault. I didn't look where I was going." I can't tell if Cecily is bruised or just shaken up by her own vulnerability. "Do you want me to take you to the doctor?"

Sitting on the seat of her walker, she's crying at the floor. She won't look at me.

"Do you want me to take you home?"

People are staring as their shopping carts roll past. God, I'm an asshole. I stopped showing up at Cecily's place and she never knew why.

She starts to catch her breath, to try to talk through tears. I think she said, "Did you tell the police?"

Behind me a man asks, "Can I help? Do you need to call someone?" He offers his cell phone.

I look at him, and at the little girl kicking her legs in the child's seat of his shopping cart. "She gots hurt?" the little girl asks.

"I think we just need some air." I don't know if Cecily has taken a turn for the worse since I last saw her.

The man smiles sympathetically and moves on down the aisle.

"She gots hurt?" the girl asks her father as they turn the corner.

"Can you stand up?" Cecily nods and I get her onto her feet, abandon my cart, and move with her toward the store exit.

The two of us come outside into the sunlight.

"You want to catch your breath for a minute?"

She snuffles and we sit down on a bench next to the store's plant nursery. I root around in my purse until I find my scruffy travel pack of tissues and put one in Cecily's hand.

She blows her nose and turns her red, watery eyes to me. "You have to know how sorry I am," she says. "I loved that little boy."

"You mean my little boy? Are you talking about Frankie?"

She crushes the tissue to her mouth and nods.

"He loved you too, Cecily." I'm confused. Maybe she's confused. "Is this why you're upset? Did you just find out?"

"He called," she says.

"Who called?"

"He told me. The baby took my pills."

I look at her. "What do you mean, the baby took your pills?"

"Did you tell the police?" she asks again.

I look down at the pavement and try to make sense of her. "Frankie . . ." To say it—it feels like trying to roll a boulder from a tomb. "He fell out of a window."

"When he took the pills?"

"No, Frankie didn't take any pills." She doesn't need to know that it was me, I'm the one who swallowed the pill the night our world blew apart. "Frankie climbed up on the windowsill. He fell."

"He said—"

"Who said?"

"A man called me. He said he was going to tell the police because of what I did. The pills."

"Frankie fell because . . . because his dad and I weren't paying attention." A tear pops and rolls down my cheek. "Not because of you, Cecily. I don't know who—"

She's only giving me snatches and it's like lightning in my head. Flashes of illumination and then nothing. *Come on, Cecily, try to remember.*

Staring out into the parking lot, I watch people load groceries into trunks, children into backseats. It all looks so simple from a distance.

"Cecily, I promise you're not in trouble. Can you start from the beginning?"

Breath shudders in her chest. "He never said his name. He phoned me at night. He said he was calling on your behalf. He said, Maggie's baby swallowed Xanax with my name on it and he died."

Calling on *my* behalf? It had to be Ben. Angry Ben, sad Ben, Ben with a gun. Ben trying to make Frankie make sense. Make Frankie someone else's fault.

Someone else should hurt.

"That's not true," I tell her.

"I thought you hated me." She puts her fingers against her eyes. "I was too scared to tell anyone. He phoned when I was sleeping. He phoned—" She starts to cry again. "The last time he called, he said they were going to kill him. He said that they were going to shoot him in the head. Someone. I couldn't—I heard the shot. He was crying and pleading for help. I didn't want anyone else to die. I called the police. They said if I gave them the number he called from—the call display—they could trace it. He had a gun. Someone had a gun. The police said they would investigate. I didn't know what to do. I'm sorry. I'm so foolish."

THIRTEEN

Ben

Where's here? Where's real? Is this real? Is this alive? Awake? Hands on his face, he rubs and rubs and then punches his head. Wake up. But there's Ben perched at the end of the couch, like a vulture. Like a goblin. "You're not real!"

"No, you're not real." A hand shoots out, takes him by the ankle, and yanks him down the hall to the woods. The hand on his ankle is a child's now and the boy drags him like a stuffed bear up the side of a hill, his flesh snagging on rock and broken branches.

At the top, Frankie stands at the edge of the cliff and looks out to the stars. "Now, you go," he says and he unzips the sky and shows the sun on the other side—blinding, screaming light. "Go, Daddy, go."

"Like this!" Frankie climbs through the gash himself. "Come! Come here, Daddy." So bright. So sweet.

Ben's too black for that bright. He's a black hole; he'd suck the day into night.

Yes or no? Yes or no, Father? Should he get in? Would they even let him in? The rip is getting smaller. Closing, closing. Choose. No?

No! It's always no! No bliss for the wicked. Jump then, just drop dead, falling and falling, scream and scream and no one hears!

Every time he jumps, he lands on the couch crying. Hell is nowhere. Hell is nothing.

Somebody help me. Wake me up. Who? Where's the fucking phone? Where's the pills? Where's a number? Cecily G. Riley? Please, help me. Mrs. Riley. I can't wake up, Mrs. Riley. Please wake me up.

Everywhere you look, there's Ben. There's naked Ben reaching, sliding the gun closer.

Look at that gun! The way the light shimmers. Beautiful. It's bright as a gash in heaven.

Put her there, Father, put the muzzle to his head. Are you listening? For chrissake, are you listening? Can you hear me? Can anyone hear me?

He's got a gun, Mrs. Riley. He's going to shoot me in the head.

Boom! Flying through space, hunting for that gash of light. It's just a keyhole now. Keyhole bright, a hole in the night.

Frankie pulling and pulling, shredding me, dragging me to the other side. Please, Daddy, please, come, come home. Take me home.

Can anybody hear me?

"I hear you, Ben." Francis. Francis is saying, "Listen to me, Ben."

It's better without Ben, so much better.

"No, Ben, it's not. If the voice you're hearing in your head says you're no good, turn from it. That is *not* the voice of God. That's not love. That is not how God speaks to us."

God, help me.

"That's right, just ask for help. Be here, Ben. Maggie needs you. Maggie loves you. *You are loved.*"

Oh God. Help me. Father. Please! Maggie, Maggie, help me, please help me.

On the floor, on my knees, Maggie's brother catching me, Francis wrapped around me like a cloak, like a cradle, saying, "I've got you, Ben. I've got you, brother."

Maggie. Maggie.

"I'm going to get her," Father says. Francis says, "I'm going to get Maggie. Talk to Maggie, Ben. She needs you. I'm calling her now."

THIRTEEN

Maggie

Poor Cecily. How could I leave her dangling like I did?

Her head buried in my neck, I'm holding her tight now, rocking her. "Oh sweetheart, I'm so sorry this happened. I wish I'd phoned you. I wish I had. But I couldn't bear to say it out loud." I rest my cheek on her head and rock and cry with her. "I think I know who called. He was scared too. He was just scared and sad. It's going to be okay."

Eventually Cecily wipes her eyes and gets her breath back. She sits up. "I thought you hated me."

My phone buzzes in my pocket. Jesus. You got some timing, Francis. "It's my brother. I'll just be a second, okay?"

Cecily nods shakily.

"Hello."

Just breathing on the other end. It sounds like tears. As if the whole world is crying right now.

"Hello?" Clutching the phone to my ear, I can feel him there. I can feel him here. "Ben?"

"Maggie?" He sounds afraid and alone—like a boy who's woken suddenly in the dark. "Maggie? Please?"

"I'm here."

"Maggie? *Maggie.* Oh Maggie, I love you. I love you so much."

Doubled over in my lap, I crouch and listen and cry and watch my tears hit the pavement one at a time.

FOURTEEN

Ben

Wrapped around me like a cloak. Francis. He's holding Maggie to my ear. My Maggie. Her voice in my head.

"Ben," she says. "Forgive me," she says. "I love you too."

Say Ben. Say love. Say forgive.

Maggie. She feels like home. I'm almost home.

Feels like I had to crawl through ten thousand nightmares, wrestle ten thousand demons to find the girl from my own neighborhood.

Eyes all around. Orderlies. No one comes near. Francis drives them off, like wolves. Like I am small and new. He's got his cool hand on my forehead now. Like a mother in a fever, like a father in a fever.

Don't let go. Don't let me go.

"I'm here," he says. "I've got you."

Maggie?

"I won't let you go," she says. "We'll be home soon. I promise."

Maggie. Maggie. Glorious Maggie.

FOURTEEN

Maggie

Maggie?" My brother's just phoned back.

"What's happening? Where's Ben?"

"He's in his room. He's quiet now." Francis lets his breath go as if he's been holding it too tight for too long. "I've never heard someone cry like that . . ."

"Should I come down?"

Cecily is beside me on the bench, holding my free hand and stroking it like a broken sparrow.

"I think he's okay," Francis says. "They gave him a sedative. Why don't we let him sleep. We'll come back tomorrow."

Tomorrow. My guts twist and clench when the call ends. I put the phone in my pocket and look at Cecily. Her face is so filled with sympathy that I lean against her, rest my head on her shoulder, and sigh and murmur, "What's to become of us?"

"We'll survive," she says. "That's what we do."

AFTER I TAKE Cecily home, I sit outside her building in Lucy's Volvo and swallow and swallow, trying to decide what to do next. Feels like I should be down at the hospital with Ben, should be upstairs in Cecily's apartment helping her do whatever it is she needs done, should be putting Lucy's car back in her garage, should be picking up Francis, should be, should be, should be.

I put the car in drive. I should at least get one thing over with.

ONCE LUCY'S CAR is back in her garage, I take her keys and head up to the fourteenth floor. Just as I get off the elevator, my phone rings again.

"Hi. It's Lucy," she says. "I just, ah, I wanted to see if you were okay." Her voice sounds small and breakable.

"I'm in your building. I'm coming down your hall right now."

"You're back?" Just ahead of me, her apartment door swings open and she holds up her phone with a fragile smile. "Isn't that funny," she says, but her voice is melancholy.

"I just wanted to drop off your keys." I hold them out and when I reach her put them in her hand.

"Oh. You're coming in, aren't you?" As I hesitate, she says, "Yes. Come in. I owe you for your time today."

"No, no. Of course you don't."

Inside, Lucy closes the door and rests her hands on her walker. The two of us stare at one another.

"Are you mad at me?" she says. "I'm sorry. I really am very sorry."

"It's not that, it's—Oh maybe it is. I am upset with you. I can't do this, Lucy."

"What do you mean?"

"Things are really upside down for me right now. I hope it's going to get better soon, but I'm not in a state of mind to—"

"Oh no." Lucy's eyes open in fear. "Maggie, please. Don't say that. I was wrong. I won't do it again. I just thought that it would be nice, that you—"

"It's not nice. It's private. It's my life. And how can this be nice for you? Throwing good money after bad, lining their pockets, these charlatans and phonies—"

"No!" Her face is a sudden storm. "You don't know what you're talking about! I never told her that—Oh forget it." She wipes her cheek and, losing her balance, grabs hold of her walker, turns it around, and shoves it toward her balcony. "A goddamn walker. I can't even walk anymore. You don't know! You're not alone. You're not scared that—"

"Not scared? For God's sake, Lucy! I have no one! I lost my child. He's gone because of me. My husband's gone because of me. And my brother's going and everyone's gone. Just like that. I hate these idiots and their phony spook talk!"

She stares out the sliding glass door for a moment and then shouts, "You have your whole life in front of you!" She turns her walker back. "I've got one foot in the grave. Every day I look at the trees and I see less and less, but I try to fill my eyes and my head and really see them because I don't have much time left. And I'm afraid. I'm afraid of lying in the cold ground." She looks down and her curved back starts to heave. "I'm afraid every time I go to sleep that I might not wake up." Tears slide off her jaw.

I look at the floor. Ben's voice sifts into my head: *Don't let go. Don't let me go.*

And then, like a canyon echo, Lucy says, "Don't go. Don't leave me."

Don't go. It's true: I can't keep leaving.

"Okay." I touch her sleeve. "I won't. We'll figure it out."

Lucy fumbles for my hand. She grabs hold and I grab back. We stand in her living room a few moments, holding hands. Holding tight.

WHEN FRANCIS COMES home, he brings Chinese takeout with him, but neither of us can stomach food right now. We are leaning against the counter of my tiny kitchen. Probably because it's the smallest room in the place, one where we can stay close without acknowledging the need to do so.

Francis turns on the cold-water tap and fills the kettle. "By the end he sounded more like himself. When I first got there, it was—it was like he was somewhere else eavesdropping on his own life."

"So he *did* shoot himself, but he wasn't trying to kill himself?"

"That's what I understood." Francis puts the kettle on the stove and turns on the burner. "He, ah—well, he did give me permission to talk about this with you, so—"

"Just tell me what happened."

"Basically, in the days or weeks leading up to that night, he hadn't slept and he took some drugs to put himself out. He fell asleep and then he couldn't escape his own nightmare.

He thought he was dreaming. He shot himself in the head to wake up." Francis shudders and stares at the creaking kettle.

"Jesus Christ." I turn to the sink and hold on to the counter's edge. "Where would he get a gun?"

"Cola. Cola was in trouble and he got himself a gun. Then he stole drugs from a veterinary clinic. Ben was holding the drugs for him."

"What? *Why?* That kid is such a *jackass.*"

"Kid. What is he, thirty?"

"So, now what? How long will he have to—"

"I'm guessing that once it's established that he's not a danger to himself, they'll probably let him go. I told Ben's doctor what happened today. What about you? How do you feel? Are you ready to . . . ?"

"If he's really *there,* I want him here." Cecily's strong old face slides to mind. "We'll survive. That's what we do."

FIFTEEN

Ben

B en," Dr. Lambert says. He's early today.

"Yes."

"You're here." Lambert's grin just about splits his face in half.

"I am." The word *I* still feels awkward. Feels like an electric shock.

We're sitting in the white, white room that doesn't look so white anymore.

What was so white, white about it?

This morning, only the sheets are white. The blanket is blue. Lambert's chair is chrome and beige. Pale green curtains frame that whole other world: willows and sky, cars and asphalt.

"How do you feel?" Lambert says.

"Awake."

Lambert nods. "Yesterday was—Dr. Raymond said that you had, well, yes, an *awakening* is a good word for it. She phoned me at home. I was delighted, Ben. I was just delighted to hear it."

"You thought I—" *I.* It echoes. Like an onus, an accusation. There's still a bandage on my head, but smaller now. "I didn't want to die. I just wanted to wake up."

To get the hell out of hell. Nobody's got a chance in hell.

"And you did." Lambert watches my face, searching. His eyes are steady. They're not fool blue. They're faith blue. Mercy blue. "You're here," he says again. "I'm glad you're alive, Ben." Lambert's voice is as gentle as peace, and its tone vibrates in my guts. "Are you?"

"I am."

Maggie

W as that the hospital?" Francis watches me.

It's just past 9 A.M.

"It was Dr. Lambert, Ben's therapist." I set my cell phone down on the windowsill. "It's like you said—they feel that Ben is no longer a danger to himself. But, before Dr. Lambert releases him, he wanted to know that Ben would be going home to someone. Family." I look out the window. I feel the urge to pace, but this apartment isn't big enough for pacing. "He could be discharged as early as this afternoon. If we're ready. He's ready. He thinks." My chest clenches.

"Who thinks?"

"Ben. And the doctor. Or he could come home tomorrow." I feel weightless and heavy at once. As if I'm roaring down the first skyscraping hill on a roller coaster.

"You don't sound so sure."

"Well, he shouldn't be alone. So—" I look across the road

to a couple of little girls drawing on the sidewalk with electric blue chalk. "And so, he should come here."

Behind me, Francis keeps watching me. I can feel him. I walk into the kitchen and stand at the counter. My eyes poke around as if I've come in here for a purpose. I tap my fingernails on the countertop. Eventually I move back into the living room and stare out the window again.

Francis is right where I left him on the couch. "Well, what'd you tell him? Yes, no? Today, tomorrow?"

"Today. At one. He said I should bring a change of clothes for him. Because the clothes that Ben arrived in are—" The little girls across the road are using neon purple chalk now. And screaming green. They're drawing beasts with big teeth and happy faces. Friendly monsters. "Which means I have to go back to the old apartment."

"Right. Do you want me to come?"

I turn and make for the coffee table, start clearing things off.

"I'm not done with that." My brother reaches out for his mug.

My hands are full of stuff and I don't know what I'm doing. I'm not done with mine either.

He takes his cup back, swirls the last of his coffee around. "I'm guessing nobody cleaned up the place after. It could be pretty . . . tough to see."

I march back to the kitchen and start washing out my coffee cup, stick it in the drying rack, and then pick up the sponge again and begin wiping surfaces. Any surfaces.

Francis calls out to me. "Just to remind you, I'm supposed to check into Our Lady of Perpetual Help tomorrow. But if

Ben's coming here tonight, I could see about going in earlier. Or I could always go back to Holy Trinity."

"No." I stop wiping. "Let's be together tonight. Okay? If you don't mind. And tomorrow—is Father Michael supposed to take you? Because I could drive you."

There's no answer for a few seconds and so I move to where I can see him.

His smile is thin and melancholy when he says, "I'd rather go with you. I could leave my car for you. You could use it while I'm gone."

Sagging against the wall, I stare at the raggedy sponge in my hands. "I don't want to go back to our place. I don't want to see it."

SUNLIGHT IS BREAKING through the clouds when we pull into the visitor parking in the back lot of the old building. I'd like to view this as some kind of cheery sign that things are getting better, but dread has got me by the throat.

In the passenger seat, Francis looks up at the apartment window. I can't do the same. I can't face that window.

"Do you want to give me the keys and I'll go up?"

I pick at a small tear in the seat of Lucy's Volvo. After we made up, she asked me to take it home again. I keep hearing her frightened voice in my head. *Don't leave me* is wrapped around Ben's *Don't let me go.* If Ben had said that to begin with, I would have stayed. I'm sure of it.

"Mags?"

"I'm coming."

"Okay. But if you want to tell me what to get, I don't mind."

"I'm coming." I open the driver's door.

The two of us climb out of the car. Francis heads for the back door of the building and I stand there looking at the pavement under our window. It's clean now. Like nothing happened. Sirens, red spinning lights, police. My skin prickles, my limbs feel gelatinous. Francis comes back and takes my hand, leads me to the back door.

We take the stairs to the third floor.

Outside my old door, I look at the raised brass suite number and then down at the keys in my hand. What if there's blood all over the living room? The false memory of a gunshot sounds off in my head and for a moment, I'm sure I'll throw up.

Francis takes the keys from me and puts one in the lock. He turns it slowly and as the door opens, he holds my hand again. "I'm with you," he says, and we walk into the front hall of my old home. A sharp smell cuts my nostrils.

"What the hell is that?" I take my hand back.

"Smells like solvent or varnish or something."

The two of us creep down the hall, past the closed bedroom door. I hold my breath as we turn the corner into the living room.

Clean. No blood. Although the couch is covered with what looks like an old drape: brown and amber, with rod pockets at one end. I don't need to know what's under that drape. Don't want to.

The venetian blinds clank as Francis opens the window. He brushes dust off his hand and heads for the little dining area outside the kitchen. I follow him and half-expect to see Ben and Frankie and me: a jar of peanut butter on the table, a bag of bread. Except I don't. There's old newspaper spread out with a small wooden box in the middle, stained blue. A couple of cans sit next to it: wood stain and polyurethane. Scattered over the rest of the table are bits of sandpaper, and rags.

The two of us stand over the box. The lid is carved with the letters BEN.

A thump from down the hall—our heads jerk toward the bedroom.

Someone hisses in frustration.

Francis and I look at one another. We head toward the noise.

Francis knocks on the bedroom door. "Hello?"

"It's me, Maggie," I say, as if that will mean something to whoever's in there. Francis turns the knob. Grabbed from the other side, the door flies open.

"You scared the shit out of me!"

Cola. He's got a tire iron in his hand.

Hand on my chest, I back up and lean against the hall wall. "How the hell did you get in here?"

"The spare," he says, clearly hurt that I would need to ask. "Ben always keeps the spare key with me."

THE THREE OF us are sitting at the table staring at the blue box. Cola's been holed up here since the night they took Ben away.

"He was so pissed with me and—and, Vera was really like, fucking mad-dog," he says. Cola has been explaining to us that he "borrowed" his girlfriend's car. He also "borrowed" some veterinary drugs from her clinic. He just needed to store the drugs with Ben for a little while. I'd like to punch

Cola right now—just punch him and punch him until I start to feel some relief.

"—so I was coming back to get my stuff," he goes on. "And then I get here and there's cops and paramedics and lights are flashing. They were loading someone into an ambulance." He blinks and fidgets with a corner of newspaper.

"I asked one of the neighbors standing on the sidewalk and he says, 'Dude committed suicide. Shot himself in the head.' I knew it was Ben. Cuz of me. I bought the gun. He did it with that. And I thought—" Tears come into Cola's eyes.

"But then I realized he couldn't be dead, you know, cuz of how they were rushing and they'd put a respirator on him. So I waited till everyone was gone and came in to see if the drugs and stuff were still here. I didn't want him to get in trouble on top of it. Except the gun was gone. I guess the cops took it. The boxes were still in the closet, though, so I brought them back to Vera's. Plus her car. She really hates my guts now. But I gave it all back!"

Cola shoves the hair out of his eyes and my brother's words echo: *Kid? What is he, thirty?*

"I don't know if the cops are going to come after me. Vera must've told them, right? Maybe. I was kind of freaking when I went down to the hospital to find out how he was. They won't say *shit* over the phone. The bullet didn't even penetrate his skull—always told him he had a hard head!" Cola smiles a little and looks away. He picks up the blue-stained box, stares at the carved letters on top. "You, um, would you give this to him?" He opens the hinged lid. Inside, it's smooth and finished with a paler blue. "He used to like when I did woodwork in school. He thought I should be a real carpenter-dude, make furniture and stuff."

"It's beautiful," Francis says. "May I?"

Cola puts the box in my brother's hands. "Buddy of mine let me use his tools. He's got a garage full of shit."

Francis opens the box again and looks closer at the inside of the lid. " 'We'll Sing in the Sunshine,' " he reads. "You carved all this?"

"That's a song we used to like when we were kids. And I want to put this in there too." Cola gets up and goes into the kitchen, returns with a clear plastic bag. He pulls out an old greeting card, folded in half. Flattening it out, he hands it to Francis. "My dad gave this to Ben for his sixteenth birthday."

I lean over my brother's shoulder. The front of the card says, "Son: On your special day I want you to know that . . ." Inside it continues, "Having a son like you is reason to be proud and thankful—not just on your birthday, but always." Underneath is some scrawled handwriting. "*Ben,*" it says. "*You're a smart, talented guy and I'm proud of you even though I don't always say it. Love, Your Old Man.*"

Cola takes the card back and looks at the inside, his lips moving as he reads. "Dad was all right when he wasn't drinking." He closes the card. "I used to feel like I disappeared when my brother came into the room. When Ben left home, I found this under his bed. And it seemed like proof, you know. Of, like, I don't know, that our dad loved us. Ben didn't seem to care about it, so I kept it. Maybe he might like it now." Cola folds it in half again and slips it into his blue Ben box.

"I'm sure he'll love it. You're an excellent craftsman," Francis says. "I can see why Ben's impressed with you."

He can see why Ben's *impressed* with him? Goddamn donkey-boy and his stolen veterinary drugs and his fucking gun. I look at my brother's big soft hands on the box, the loving, appreciative way he runs a finger over the corners.

I can't find it in myself to say something kind. I want to smack Cola. Tell him to grow up. "So why are you here? Vera kicked you out? You get kicked out of your own place too?"

Cola keeps his eyes away from mine. "I owe a guy some money. That's why I bought the gun. Because this guy was going to . . . And then Ben gave me—he borrowed a thousand bucks from the old man and I tried to bring it to the guy as a down payment. Show of good faith, you know. Turned out the guy got arrested for assault and battery. Bought me some time."

Cola rolls an edge of newspaper between his fingers and then finally meets my eyes. "I know I fucked up. It's not like I don't *know*. But I called the hospital and they told me Ben's out today. Dad's getting out at the end of the week. Maybe it's like a second chance for us."

My anger is getting stringy, turning into something like pity, and I'm not sure what to do with any of it. I wait for Francis to say something. He's better at that stuff.

The dead air drags on. My brother's leaving me on the hook this time. Finally I say, "Do you want to come to the hospital with us?"

Cola takes a breath and then takes another before he says, "I'm going to get on a bus this afternoon. Buddy of mine says he can get me a job doing construction out west. He says he can get me into an apprenticeship program." Cola shoots a hopeful glance at Francis. "And then I'd be a certified tradesman."

"Sounds like a wonderful opportunity," my brother says. He sets the box on the table and we all look at it.

The carved letters are so smooth and exacting, it seems impossible that the jerk sitting across from me had anything to do with their creation. If there weren't sandpaper and wood dust all over the floor, I'd have been worse than skeptical.

"Yeah, that sounds, um—I'll tell Ben," I say. "He'll be . . ." And I pause, wrestling with the word. "He'll be proud of you."

Cola's face brightens. He smiles and he nods as if he can't think of a better outcome.

SIXTEEN

Ben

Sitting on the skinny, blue-blanket bed, waiting. She'll be here any minute. Maggie. Ben's sweet Maggie. My Maggie. I liked Ben a little better when he was far away. When the lights were on but he wasn't home. Now he's going home in a box and I am that box.

Lambert said his goodbyes this morning. Shook my hand, grabbed my shoulders. Embrace me, my sweet embraceable you. I am his pet project. Star pupil. A star in a jar. Feels like I've been shot from a cannon, aimed at a jigger of water, and here I sit with my nose against the glass, waiting.

Tap at the door.

Look who's here: Gwen. Blessed Gwen. Disappearing Gwen.

"Hi," she says. She shines her nervous gaze straight at me. As if she can see, hear, and smell through my glass. See my willing spirit and my weak flesh.

"Hello." That's all I can come up with. Was it this hard to speak before? Actions speak louder than words and mine have been deafening. Yet, here's Gwen. No one in the room, but me, and still she's here.

"I'm going home today," she says. "I wanted to say goodbye and thank you for, for—" She looks away. Words are hard. Hard as hell. Hard as the back of God's head. "For listening to me," she finally says. "And for sharing your friend—your priest friend—it meant a lot to me."

"Yeah. He's ah, he's my—" *Deliver your servant, Gwen, from every sorrow* . . . Maybe it worked, a little deliverance. You can see clear into Gwen's eyes today: acid eyes. Burn-through-it-all eyes. It must hurt to see so much. "You've got eyes like my Maggie."

Gwen looks up, raises those torches of hers as if they're heavy lifting. "Your Maggie?" A little smile melts across her lips and she says, "You love her."

You got no idea, Gwen. "I'm leaving today too."

"Your Maggie is coming," she says. She says it like a prophecy. A revelation. The way Maggie herself would. "You'll be okay," Gwen says. "We'll be okay."

Are you sure, Gwen? How can you be? Like a mind reader, she takes a step forward. Her hands rise from her sides, just enough to cue me, get me on my feet.

I take hold of her hands, her mother hands, and we stand in the middle of the room, listening to our hearts thump and the squawk and chatter of every lost soul still wandering the halls.

"Ben?" Maggie. Maggie's at the door. The way she says Ben—like it's a nice place to be.

"It's you," I say. "You're here."

Her kaleidoscope eyes shift and turn at the sight of Gwen's hands releasing mine.

Gwen turns to her. "You're Maggie." She extends a hand. "I'm Gwen. I'm glad to have met you before I leave. You're just like I imagined."

"Oh." Her eyes meet Gwen's and soften. As if Gwen's told her a secret. Maggie shakes her hand.

"I guess this is it." Gwen looks back, right at the holes where Ben's eyes are now. "Be well. Let's all be well."

Maggie watches her go. Then she looks down at the bag in her hands. She looks at me. And then away again, around the room.

Don't look away. Please don't look away. I won't if you won't.

Scared to touch her now. Scared she might pull away. "You're here." I say it again, say it the way Lambert said it to make sure. Make it real.

"I brought you some clothes." She reaches for the sleeve of my hospital pajamas, as if she might touch me, but stops.

Look at me again. Pin me to the earth, Maggie. How can I be Ben, if I'm not your Ben?

She looks at the black hole, the bandage, the reason we're here.

"And I saw Cola today," she says. "He wanted me to give you something. It's in here." She puts the paper shopping bag in my hand and the graze of her fingers sends a sharking blue jolt up my veins.

She pulls her hand back.

Inside the bag: It's a box, letters carved into the lid. Have to sit down for this. Sit on the bed.

Smooth and light in my hands. Beveled and blue. BEN, it says. Calls my name like a little boy. Like he would love me forever. "Where is he?"

"He's out of town."

"Oh yeah?" Look at this thing. Smooth as a pup's ear. "Huh. He's a talented little fuck."

A smirk from my Maggie. A sniff of laughter. "Yeah. Maybe he'll—he had a job offer, an apprenticeship program he said. He's, um, he feels terrible. About what happened."

Raise the lid. Cola's carved the inside too. *We'll Sing in the Sunshine:* Cola's prayer.

And something else. "What's this? A bill?" It's an old birthday card, yellowed with rough silver sparkles that spell "Son."

Son?

Son: On Your Special Day. Here we go down a rabbit hole. Down the old man's hidey-hole. *Ben,* it says. *Love, Your Old Man,* it says.

Jesus. Where the hell did Cola find this?

Maggie's watching, waiting. Should tell her what I remember. "There was a piece of paper inside when he gave it to me. It said 'This voucher entitles the bearer to six free driving lessons.' He even managed to give me one."

I stare some more at the scrawl at the bottom. *I'm proud of you. Love, Your Old Man.*

Cola's been holding on to this. Like a promise. Like a hope.

THE EXIT DOORS buzz and it feels like another jolt of electricity when they open. Nathan, the orderly, wheels my chair out of the psych ward and into the main hall. The free hall. Free fall. Maggie walks beside the chair. Her face is all nerves and twitch. Like we're working without a net. We are.

Cola's box sits in my lap. Velvety smooth. Rub it like a genie bottle; rub it for luck; rub it for faith.

Black phones on the wall, along the hall, they've got no keypads on them. Hospital house phones.

"Hey, Nathan, you want to do me a favor? Pick up one of these phones and find out what room Ben Brody is in?"

Not a word from Nathan. Poor old Nathan. Can feel him tense, feel him trade looks with Maggie.

"Senior," she tells him. "Ben Brody Sr. is his dad. The middle name's Stanley if they ask."

"Oh right, I gotcha," says Nathan. "You wanna stop and say hey to your pop." He coasts up to the next phone, picks up the receiver, and slumps on the wall like he knows a long wait is coming.

Maggie's eyes flick from the elevators to the floor. She doesn't want to see the old man. Maybe she doesn't want to see any of us. Who could blame her? Maybe she's going to dump me at the dump and leave it at that.

"Are you taking me back to the apartment?"

Her lips flutter. A wet butterfly. "Not the ah, not our . . . I'm taking you to my place."

Nathan hangs up the phone. "Room 3126," he says.

"I can take him down," Maggie offers. "You don't have to—"

"Oh, yes, I do have to. I got to take my man, here, all the way out the front doors. Hospital regulations."

MAGGIE AND NATHAN wait in the hall outside 3126. Two other patients in the room, both old men, both sleeping. My old man is in bed C, his eyes fixed on the window. His teeth are in. No restraints on him anymore. Hands free, feet free. Everybody's free now.

Box in hand, I stand by his bed, and look outside to the trees, look where he's looking. His head turns. He starts.

"Jesus Christ." His hand jumps and grips the bed rail. "Ben." He stares, looks at the bandage. "They said you—" Thin lips clamp shut like he can't say what they said. "You look good."

Rub the box. Rub the box for hope. "Thanks. I, ah, I even got a get-well present from your other son."

The old man takes it in his shaky hands, stares at it. "Look at that. That's nice. What is it?"

Inside, the old birthday card is knocking, it's kicking at the hinges. Or maybe that's just the echo of Miriam. My mother and her very pretty singing voice.

He opens the lid. He looks at the silver sparkles on the card. His card: son.

He eyes his own handwriting, head shaking like a big "no" to time and space and hurt. "No" to it all.

Seconds hang thick.

He keeps looking, his own words trembling in his knotted hands. Mouth open, my old man turns his watery eyes to me. "Ben," he says. Whispers it. Mouths it. His fingers grip hard and crush the card to his chest.

SIXTEEN

Maggie

I type, "Ben stopped to see his dad. Down in 5," into my phone and hit SEND.

Nathan, the orderly, watches my hands with a bored sigh.

I look at my cell and then back at him. "Sorry, is this okay? Using my phone here?"

"You're not supposed to, but . . ." He shrugs. "S'mostly intensive care, they don't like it. Messes with the monitors."

My phone buzzes. A text from Francis: "At gas station. Security kicked me out of the pickup zone."

Shit. He shouldn't be driving. I've got him babysitting Lucy's car. Goddamn hospitals charge a limb for parking.

Nathan leans against the wall. He winks at a young nurse who passes. Something she does in return makes him laugh. I lean around the doorway to get a look inside the room, see what Ben and his father are up to. All I can see is Ben's back, his hands on the bed rail.

Careful. You don't want to be invited in.

Used to feel like a punch in the heart to see Ben try to be a son to that old bastard. The first time Ben held Frankie—the look in his eyes, the roar of love like white-water rapids—I wondered how he was capable of it. The way he grew up, you'd think he'd have shut down long ago. I guess he did, eventually. Losing Frankie must have been the last straw.

"Okay, I'm ready."

It's Ben. Nathan and I jerk out of our daydreams.

"Ready to roll, man?" Nathan takes hold of the wheelchair handles.

Ben's got Cola's blue box in his hands. He holds it close like an amulet, a rabbit's foot. I can't quite read his eyes. They look more wistful coming out of his father's room than they did going in. I wonder what Old Misery-Guts said to him.

Ben gives me a light smile as he sets himself back in the chair. I return the expression. Polite. We are like cordial neighbors. After that phone call yesterday, the crying love, as if Ben were falling into my arms, I imagined that somehow, when I saw him, it would be easy between us. Instead every word feels stilted, as if we don't know exactly who we are to one another—like second cousins, twice removed.

In the elevator, I send a quick text to Francis to let him know we're almost there. I look at Ben's hands in his lap, holding the box.

Gwen? Who was she? She held his hands. She did it like she'd done it before. She did it like she was his friend, his confidante. *She held his hands.*

On the ground floor, I walk alongside, watching Nathan's

hands on my husband's wheelchair. Part of me wants to shove Nathan out of the way, as if he's just one more barrier. One more confidant. "Nice day for getting out," Nathan says.

"Sure is," I say, Ben says. Cordial and polite.

Through the front doors, I can see Lucy's Volvo pull up. Francis leans and waves, gets out of the driver's side, and runs around to the passenger's side.

The hospital doors glide open as we come close and the fresh air rushes my face, clear and bracing.

"Here you go, man." Nathan stops the chair just outside the doors. "You have a good one," he says as Ben gets up.

Ben shakes Nathan's hand, thanks him.

Nathan wheels the chair back inside and the two of us stand there, staring at his retreat as if we're lost without him.

A car honks and Ben flinches. Must feel strange, the sudden noise and bustle.

Francis comes over to us. He takes Ben's hand and shakes it. Gently. "Good to see you, brother! Welcome back."

"You, too, man." Ben looks away and I wonder if he feels embarrassed, naked in front of Francis now. In front of the world.

Francis claps his hands together as if we're about to embark on a wonderful adventure. Then he turns and jumps into the backseat.

Ben gets into the passenger seat up front and I stand here in a fog until it dawns on me to go around and get behind the wheel.

"Whose wheels?" Ben's voice is quiet and wondering as he does up his seat belt.

"One of my ladies," I tell him. I don't know if he hears me, his eyes flicking around at people and cars. "You okay?"

He starts, as if I've given him a poke. "Sure. I'm—yeah. Just a little ah—" He pulls his elbows close in a pantomime of vulnerability. "Been inside too long, I guess."

"I feel like that if I'm in the house for a couple of days even," Francis says. "Get outside and I'm jumpy as a whore in church."

"Oh, Father Luke." I put the car in drive. "Your gentility is only surpassed by your vulgarity."

"My *crudité*, as we say in France. I'm huge in France."

Ben gives a soft snort. I wonder if we're trying too hard.

SEVENTEEN

Ben

Maggie's place. It smells like Maggie and not-Maggie. Someone else's furniture. Someone else's dishes. Seems like Francis has been staying here.

Maggie's bedroom. The bed is kiddie-width. Her brother calls it the Monk's Cell.

"Maybe you guys should take the pullout tonight," Francis says. "A little more space. Tomorrow you'll have the place to yourselves."

Maggie shoots him a look, shuts him up. Protecting me? Or Francis?

"I thought we'd just slide my top mattress onto the floor," she says. "Um, and then we'd, ah, it'd be a double bed." Double bed. It hangs in the air like a bad smell. Who'd want to sleep with a man who put a bullet in his head?

"We got you some more clothes," she blurts. "Underwear and shirts, another pair of jeans. Bottom two drawers."

The dresser is in the closet. No room for it in the Monk's Cell.

Now what? Nowhere to look. Nowhere where Ben is not.

"Okay. Ah, I'm just going to—" I jab a thumb toward the bathroom. Let me in there. Let me breathe. Let them breathe. Don't hold your breath.

Bathroom door closed, it's just me and the mirror. The black hole sighs. Man in the mirror. Man in the moon. Ben and not Ben. Me and not me. Wave at Ben and Ben waves back.

The bandage is small and fresh and white. A nurse put a new one on this morning. You could probably go without, she said, but it's nice to go home with a fresh change.

Go without? Peel back the tape and look at the hole. Scabbed in a thick blood-black, it's framed with a bouquet of yellow-green bruise.

Wake up, wake up, please wake up. Blood streaming down, off my jaw, down my shirt, across the couch.

Ben shudders in the mirror, shakes his head at me. At us. "Dumb fuck."

Put the bandage back where you found it.

Sitting on the back of the toilet are the only hints of what used to be Maggie and me, bits of us in a little clay bowl: earrings, a beaded hair clip, jeweled barrettes. I bought her most of it. She likes that stuff. I like her in it. Her red-and-orange headband sits beside the bowl. Maggie's turban. It stretches in my hand, stretches me, turns me over, floats me into Christmas, before the apartment on Williams Street, before Frankie was born. Our first Christmas together? Second? One of Maggie's old ladies had given her a Deepak Chopra book. Cover-to-cover daffodils; a platitude for every occasion.

She pulled the turban on and slid it back over her hair. Sitting cross-legged with a pole-straight spine, she turned her acid eyes my way and read from the book. "Ben," she said, "you were created to be completely loved and completely lovable, for your whole life. This is what I am telling you."

"Is that supposed to be an Indian accent?" Those eyes of hers could burn a hole in your skin. *Completely loved, completely lovable.* Little did she know. This is a face only a mother could love. And even she skipped town. Maggie kept looking at me, grinning like a love-shaped lunatic. *Completely lovable. For your whole life.* Nothing to do but brush it off: "You are stone-cold racist, sister!"

"Oh no, Ben!" She laughed and bobbled her head. "This is not so. The less you open your heart to others, the more your heart suffers."

I made a microphone out of my thumb and pushed in for an interview. "Mr. Chopra, what would you say to critics who feel you're completely full of chapati?"

"Let me put it to you this way, Ben." Another head bobble, swallowing the giggles. "These skeptics, this band of bastards, need a tap in the tikka. No joke, Ben. Serious business. They need a pop in the paneer, a shot—"

Rap at the door. My Christmas movie snags and fades to black.

"Are you okay in there?" Maggie asks.

Am I okay? Look in the mirror. Are you okay? Smooth the bandage over the black hole. "Yup. Be out in a sec."

DINNER ON THE couch. Just pasta. Just simple. Francis sits on a cushion on the floor. The two of them tell stories, their stories, childhood stories. They laugh. I try.

I'm here and I'm not here. Nose against the glass. Ben in a bottle. I don't know how to play. I don't know how to find her. "You ever read that Deepak Chopra book anymore?"

The two of them turn their heads. Laughter trickles away. What the hell has that got to do with the price of eggs?

"I was just thinking of that Christmas. Who gave you that book?"

Maggie thinks for a second. "Cecily."

She looks at me; she looks at the monster. *Have I reached Mrs. Cecily G. Riley?* She knows. I probably should be in a bottle, corked and tossed.

SEVENTEEN

Maggie

It takes about three hot seconds to show Ben around the apartment and then we're left staring at each other.

Francis takes a seat on the couch. Ben stands in the middle of the room as if he's not sure about that couch business. He eyes the chairs at the little table by the window.

I ask if anyone would like something to drink. "There's juice, water, coffee, milk?" At *milk,* a clunky ha-ha comes out of me and echoes around the room. Jesus.

"I'm good with water," Ben says.

My brother rests an arm along the back of the couch as though he's very relaxed. "I'll have coffee if you're making it," he says.

I escape to the kitchen, turn on the cold-water tap, and stare at the steady stream a few moments. I never would have imagined feeling this way with Ben. Every word, every movement we make feels so precise and judicious. Francis too. All of us, careful-careful-careful—like three drunks trying to play sober.

I fill a glass with water and then start on the coffee. Then I hear Francis open his big mouth. "Maybe you guys should take the pullout tonight," he says. "A little more space." Like it's nothing, he adds, "Tomorrow you'll have the place to yourselves."

Snatching the water glass off the counter, I head back into the living area and give him a look. "I thought we'd just slide my top mattress onto the floor." My voice is full of brittle cheer.

Ben is now seated in a chair he has placed kitty-corner to the couch. I put the glass in his hand and the surprise of touching his fingers sends me babbling about the extra clothes I brought for him, extra underwear in the bottom two drawers—in the dresser—in the closet—blahblahblah.

When I run out of steam, the room is crushingly still.

Ben sets his water on the coffee table and excuses himself to go to the bathroom.

The moment the door closes Francis jumps up and yanks me into the kitchen.

"What was that?" he whispers. "Why can't I say that I'm leaving tomorrow?"

"Because—I don't know." I glance into the living room toward the bathroom door. "Because then he's going to ask why and we'll have to talk about your drunken viral video crap."

"So?"

"So I want him to feel like he's come home to a stable family, okay."

"Oh please, the Manson Family had more stability than this one."

"Fine," I hiss at him. "Say what you want then." I wrap my arms up over my head as if debris is falling from above. "Do you really have to go tomorrow?"

Francis leans against the stove. "Yes." He sighs. He takes his cell phone out of his pocket and then stuffs it back. "That Katie Wilks from the *Herald* keeps leaving me messages. And I know—it's my own fault. I just need to disappear for a while."

"You and whose army?" I look back through the living room again. "What's taking him so long? What's he doing in there?"

"I need a cigarette. Do you think Ben would mind if I smoked?"

How am I going to do this? Why, Francis? Why can't you just stay?

Ben

It's nearly midnight. Maggie found a dozen things for the three of us to watch on TV. A dozen reasons to keep our mouths shut and the lights on. Her brother finally gave us the heave. He needed the couch; it was his bedtime.

The mattress and box spring are side by side now. We've put sheets on both. Blankets. Pillows. The room is all bed. Can't even open the door all the way. She keeps finding more to do.

Pajamas on. Her old ones, red plaid. She put them on in the bathroom.

Water—we both need water, Maggie says, and she's gone again, slipping out sideways through the little space left. Slipping through the cracks.

Must have water. We had the hell, it's time for high water. Suppose it's time for Ben's pill too. Bottle's in my pocket. Pills rattle against plastic. *Have I reached Mrs. Cecily G. Riley? Who gave you that book?* Of course it was old Cecily. Who else?

Maggie's hand pokes back through the door with a cold, sweating glass. She sidesteps in. Sock-footed, she stands on my mattress with a glass in each hand and watches.

Hold them up for display: *Benjamin Brody. One tablet at bedtime.*

"Water wings," I tell her. She doesn't know what that means, asshole. Try making sense. "They're antidepressants. Lambert said they'd be like water wings till I got back on my feet."

"Yeah, that's a good idea. Makes sense, right? I mean, you know, tons of people take antidepressants, so, that's um . . . totally fine." She smiles like a nurse with a loaded bedpan. "Could you?" She hands over the waters.

I fit hers onto the little nightstand.

Her gaze follows my hand, and the glass. She looks back out the door to the dark living room.

"You don't have to close the door," I tell her. "If you don't want."

Maggie shrugs. She closes the door.

She wobbles her way across the mattress, sits on the box spring, and watches me sip back the pill with water. Watches me swallow.

"I—" I need to say this. She needs to know this. "I didn't want, ah—I wasn't trying to kill myself."

She shakes her head no. Of course not.

"I thought . . ." Eyes down. It's bright in here. Too much. Too naked.

Maggie the mind reader: She leans and switches off the lamp. "Better?" She whispers it, like a dream. She crawls under the covers on her side.

Listen to the sheets against Maggie.

A tiny inhalation from her, as though she might speak, and then she stops.

Quiet plays against the walls. Say Ben. Say we. Say us. I'm almost home.

Another little breath and she says, "Ben?"

Answer. Say something, Ben. Say what you mean. Say who you are. "Yeah?"

Maggie's hand slips through the dark and finds my face. Touches my skin. "I never stopped loving you."

"Thank you." Whisper it, say it, sing it. "Thank you, thank you, thank you."

I cup her palm to my mouth and inhale, let it melt against my face in the dark. Reach up past her wrist, up her arm to her neck, the soft of her cheek, the warm home of Maggie's face.

Tears in her throat now, my Maggie slides over, closer, onto this mattress onto Ben, onto me. She lays her arms over me, her hips against mine.

Her breath in my ear fills my head, fills the black hole with light. Her hands slide my shirt up, slide her own up, so that we are skin to skin, dissolving, liquefying.

Breathing Maggie's breath, breathing Maggie.

She, me, I—and soon I don't know where she begins and I end.

EIGHTEEN

Maggie

"You're sure? Do you want to go back in and get a snack or something for later?"

"It's a one-hour drive, Mags. I think I'll make it." Francis flicks the ash off his cigarette out the rear window of the car. He gives Ben an exaggerated look of I-Don't-Envy-You-Pal.

The day is warm and the sky so blue, it's indigo. A mass of sunlit leaves and chirping sparrows flit through the branches overhead. It's all so sweet smelling, so sweet looking, it's as though the afternoon were engineered for optimism. I'm grateful for it.

We've decided to take Lucy's car—more room for a longish drive. I get into the driver's seat. Ben buckles up on the passenger side. He knows the whole sordid story now. Francis told him over breakfast.

Francis, of course, turned it into a one-man show as he's wont to do. Ben listened with his leg against mine, his foot against mine. He listened like a man who's been there, who knows fear when he hears it.

Twenty-four hours ago, I couldn't see today coming, couldn't imagine the fear letting up. Looking back, it feels as though I had to turn out the lights to see his face, crawl into silence to hear his voice.

All morning, my head has reverberated with flashes of Ben's hands in my hair, gentle on my cheek, on my back. Holding each other again. Holding on for dear life. Holding on for forgiveness.

Every time he rests his eyes on me now, there is a rush of love through my chest, in my throat, and I'm not scared anymore. We'll survive. That's what we do.

In the backseat, Francis takes a deep drag off his cigarette and prattles on. He's been smoking and talking nonstop since he woke. "I think he was relieved, frankly. That's him all over. I remember when he was going in for surgery last year and I said, 'Oh, is he finally getting that spine transplant? Good for him.' That poor man, I shouldn't—"

I look at him in the rearview mirror. "Who are you talking about?"

"Sorry, was I interrupting your nap, dear? It's illegal for narcoleptics to drive, you know."

"Really? Well, fratricide's illegal, too, but I'm a rebel."

"Oh Lord, deliver me," Francis says, exactly like our mother used to. With a little saliva on his finger, he taps out his expiring cigarette and drops the butt into his shirt pocket. "I was talking about Father Michael. I called him yesterday. I don't think he was looking forward to depositing me at the rehab center. My spiritual director, everybody, let's give him a warm round of applause."

"*He's* your spiritual director? That squirmy little worm couldn't direct traffic."

Beside me Ben is grinning. The sight of his smile, the light in his face is like a shooting star in my guts.

Francis goes on. "He asked me if I'd like to take some classes when I get out. I said, 'I'd like to get my canon law degree, but I feel like my brain is fried. I could probably do a PhD in spirituality. I could handle fluff.' Silence. I could almost hear his little eyes blinking. Oh well, I've said worse. Google me." He pulls out his pack of Camels and lights a new one.

We keep on like that for another forty minutes or so. The closer we get to my brother's destination, though, the quieter it gets in the backseat. I watch him in the rearview mirror. The bravado is slowly replaced with a lonesome stare as he watches the traffic and trees fly by.

OUR LADY OF Perpetual Help Rehabilitation Center is surrounded by a thick moat of tall, leafy trees. An open-armed statue of Christ greets us as we nose into the circular driveway in front.

"Where's the parking lot?" I wonder out loud. "I guess we just go—"

"No, no, here is fine," Francis says, and so I stop. Window open, his face is upturned, looking from the portico to the center's brick façade, all the way up the bell tower to the tall white cross on top.

My brother's voice is soft when he says, "I think I'd like to do this on my own."

"Are you sure?"

Francis gathers his things and opens the back door.

Ben looks into his lap a moment, takes a deep breath, and then gets out too.

The three of us stand beside the car, looking up at the building. Francis glances back at the car. His mouth pulls down as he rummages for cigarettes. He shakes the empty pack and then crumples it.

I hold out my hand and take it from him.

"Okay . . . well," Francis says. "I guess this is it." He extends a hand to Ben.

Ben takes hold. "Thank you, Francis. For everything." He throws his arm around my brother's back and claps him close. "You'll get through this, brother."

"You're welcome. Always." Francis's voice trembles slightly.

He turns from Ben and takes both of my hands in his. "Well, sweetheart. Thank you for taking me in. For taking me here." He puts his arms around me and we hold each other tight. "You have no idea how much you mean to me," he murmurs in my ear. "I love you."

My throat is clenched and it's hard to make real sound. A whisper is easier. "I love you too."

Over Francis's shoulder, I watch a smile smooth across Ben's face and the sinking sun casts a light that brings out the gentle, liquid blue of his eyes.

My brother and I let each other go. As Francis steps back he says, "Oop, you've got a—" He peers at my cheek.

"—eyelash," Ben says. "Hold still." Ben touches my face.

When he takes his hand back there's a tiny hair on his thumb. "Make a wish." He holds it out for me.

"Maybe you should take this one," I tell my brother.

"Won't work for me," he says. "It's yours."

I glance from Ben to Francis and, for a flicker of a moment, I wonder at the difference between a wish and a prayer. We plead for help from eyelashes, dandelions, pennies, wishbones, and shooting stars. And then some of us have the nerve to get down on our knees and clasp our hands. What must it be like to be so brave and bereft at once? To drop all one's defenses? It's one thing when a chicken bone is deaf to your deepest desires, but it must be something else when God goes silent.

Taking Ben's wrist, I hold his thumb, close my eyes, and blow the eyelash toward the sun.

Acknowledgments

So many people helped to bring this fictional world to life but none more than Timothy Kelleher. I cannot imagine having written *The Crooked Heart of Mercy* without your unending encouragement, astute observations, and your deep bright love. You bring my real world to life.

My family, as always, is my rock and a constant revelation: Irene Livingston, you are an ever-flowing font of inspiration and a force to be reckoned with! Thank you. Lenore Angela, your thoughts and memories of being a seniors' hand-for-hire helped to make Maggie's life feel real. Barbara Kelleher, your recollections of a missing mother and a lost childhood contributed more to these characters than you will ever know.

There were details needed for this story that often required a particular expertise and I have many experts to thank. Enormous gratitude goes to Dr. Helen Schwantje from BC Wildlife Management for your generosity and willingness to ponder a pharmaceutical that would suit my purposes—it had to be common, yet unusual, sleep-inducing yet hallucinogenic, and it had to be available in U.S. veterinary clinics. You made it work! My thanks as well to Dr. David A. Johnson at GlaxoSmithKline—the thought you put into your letters and your opinions on the logistics of designer drugs proved invaluable.

Writing about a Catholic priest takes a very specific kind of inside familiarity. Fortunately, I had the opportunity to spend time with several seminarians and priests, but I must extend a special thank you to Joseph Kury who allowed me to quiz him, pester, and poke him about his experiences, both personal and vocational. You are a rare bird, Joey.

Theological devotion has long held a fascination for me and I am a church-hopper from way back, but the Church of Spiritualism was one I had not encountered in person before now. I'm indebted to the people of the First United Church of Spiritualism and the International Spiritualist Alliance—thank you for your welcoming souls and comfortable pews.

A big shout of thanks must also go to the BC Arts Council for its generous financial support. You made it easier to breathe.

And finally, I must thank the team who brought this book into the world. To my Canadian editor, Anne Collins: You are brilliant, fierce, and magnificent and I have been impossibly lucky to have you on my side all these years. My outstanding U.S. editor Emily Krump: In this, our inaugural collaboration, your keen insights brought leaven to a difficult topic; your embrace of this book will remain precious to me always. Grainne Fox, what can I say—I had no idea that such a creature as you existed: a literary agent with a superb mind, a steel spine, and a heart as big as all get-out. I am thankful, too, that you brought Rachel Crawford into the fold. Rachel, you were always on the case with great smarts, huge diligence and a sense of humor just when I needed it. What a clan to have around me; I'm so very glad to have found you all.

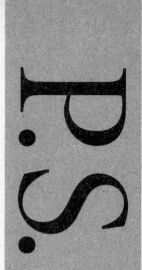

Insights,
Interviews
& More . . .

Meet Billie Livingston

Author photograph by Braden Haggerty.

BILLIE LIVINGSTON is the award-winning author of three novels, a collection of short stories, and a poetry collection. Her most recent novel, *One Good Hustle,* a *Globe and Mail* Best Book selection, was nominated for the 2012 Giller Prize and for the Canadian Library Association's Young Adult book of the year. Her short story "Sitting on the Edge of Marlene" has been adapted into a feature film and debuted at the Vancouver International Film Festival, and a second feature based on Livingston's short fiction is currently in preproduction. She lives in Vancouver, British Columbia. ◌

www.billielivingston.com

@BillieLiving

The Story Behind *The Crooked Heart of Mercy*

WHEN PEOPLE FIND OUT that I'm a writer, the question they ask again and again is, "Where do you get your stories?" Since writing *The Crooked Heart of Mercy*, I'm tempted to tell them, "There's an app for that!" Sort of. Let me explain. . . .

For three years I was haunted by three strangers skulking in the shadows of my mind: Francis, an alcoholic priest with little interest in celibacy; Ben, a man with a hole in his head; and Maggie, a woman who's lost her child. I had no idea what one had to do with the others.

Francis, the priest, showed up early on and in the most obvious way: exposure. Ten years ago, my husband was in a seminary in Washington, D.C. When we were first dating, I used to visit him there. Many a night was spent on the rooftop patio drinking cocktails and bantering with young men who felt that they had a vocation, but were unsure if they could put their appetites aside. Much of their fear, grace, and smart-assed playfulness crystallized in Francis.

Ben started nosing around after I had read about a seventeen-year-old boy in Florida who ate too many psychedelic mushrooms, fell asleep, and very nearly killed himself in his desperation to wake up. But Ben was a different animal: a thirty-something limo driver with a sharp mind and an acid tongue. The hole in his head was the darkest, angriest ▶

part of him. The hole would come from a nightmare and the nightmare would become the hole.

But who was Maggie? Early on, her voice was like a bad phone connection where I could only hear every third word. Ben was swiftly becoming the loudest of the three. I was convinced that if I could crack open Ben's mind and find his nightmare, I could crack the story and find my way to Maggie and Francis.

I decided to try writing a short story in Ben's voice.

A little stuck, I went for a long walk to let my mind drift. Eventually, it all rushed in—Ben's dark dream, existential and creepy. Panicked, I opened my cell phone to dictate a few words to Siri, the voice-to-text app. *"Ben is sucked back through his own eye sockets,"* I said. *"The eyes of the planet, the eyes of God! Falling through the air in a rush of embryonic sludge, he lands with a squelch. . . ."*

I tapped DONE, stared at the phone, and waited for it to transcribe my words. The little blue wheel turned and turned as the app worked. It seemed to take forever. (Was the din of traffic too loud?) Finally, Siri finished. I looked at the phone, expecting to read my thoughts on the screen. Only one word was there: *Family.*

I snorted. Some transcription. More like a translation!

Siri, channeling the sarcasm of the gods, had unlocked the whole thing.

Ben, Maggie, Francis: *family*. What else? Ben is married to Maggie. The lost child was theirs together. Francis, the priest with the lousy grip on celibacy, is Maggie's brother. And Maggie is just as lippy and lively, playful and broken as Francis. Like all families, they know just how to push each other's buttons. Of course they do, they installed them.

I often write about family, the ones we're born into, the ones we choose, and the ways one so often affects the other.

My real-life family frequently laces through my fictional families. Threads of dialogue, bits of history. That little boy, Ben and Maggie's lost child—he's from an old family memory, a story that is and isn't my own. Years before I came along, my father and his first wife had a little boy. The boy fell out of a window and died at the age of two. For years I have been haunted by a child I never met, a boy who would have been my brother. I've wondered how his mother recovered from the shattering loss of one distracted moment. Now that boy is Frankie, the child of Ben, a man with a hole in his head, and Maggie, a woman with a hole in her heart. He is also the namesake of his uncle Francis, a priest so flawed and yet gifted with a kind of grace that helps people forward with the weight of their own secret burdens.

Family drives my fiction. Who else do we love so deeply, so keenly, and at the same time in such a roughshod way? In the belly of family is where we learn ▶

how to fear and hope. We cling to family and run from them. Even when they feel like strangers, they are imprinted on our hearts as well as in our DNA. I write about family because they are universal; they are us. ༄

Reading Group Guide

1. "How do you fill a hole? If you take from the whole to fill a hole, is anything made whole?" How do Ben's words reflect the themes of trauma and recovery in the novel?

2. Both Ben and Maggie feel extremely guilty over Frankie's death. How do they deal with this guilt in their everyday lives?

3. Given that Maggie shows disdain for religion many times during the novel, why do you think she turns to the church in her times of need? (For instance, when it concerns her son.)

4. Why did the author choose to have the narrative jump back and forth between different time lines and events? How does this serve the novel and how would it be different if it read chronologically?

5. Why does Lucy find such solace in the United Church of Spiritualism? Why does this bother Maggie?

6. According to psychologists, dissociation from reality is a coping mechanism for dealing with extreme stress or grief and can manifest in different ways. In what ways do Ben and Maggie each dissociate?

7. Do you think that Ben's dissociation existed before his self-injury and hospital stay? When and why do you think it started? ▶

8. Does Francis feel guilt regarding his sexual orientation or is he comfortable with who he is? Where do you think his tendency toward substance abuse originated?

9. In what ways does the author use the narrative voice to connect the reader to Ben's experience? Do you think that Ben is a more or a less reliable narrator when he is outside of his own body?

10. How are the themes of religion and spirituality explored in the novel? Discuss the differences between the characters who are more religious and those who are more spiritual.

11. The chapters of the novel alternate between the narratives of Maggie and Ben. The time lines of their respective narratives do not coincide until one of the very last chapters. How do you think this relates to the development of the characters and their relationship?

12. Ben and Cola each have very complicated relationships with their father. Do you think they love him or do they simply feel obligated toward him? Why?

13. How do Ben and Maggie each figure out that they need each other to heal from their emotional trauma? Did Dr. Lambert play any part in Ben's recovery?

14. How does Ben's view of the physical world change when he comes out of his dissociative state? How does his attitude change? Why do you think this is?

15. At the end of the novel, are Ben and Maggie finally "made whole"? ◌